Chapter One

For a while, all I could do was sit there and stare at her. Granted, I had been staring at her for months, but that night was different. She was different, but I guess I was too. I shifted a little on the spot where I sat on the floor and ignored the broken glass underneath me. A cool night breeze poured in from the window and I remember that it felt good against my head. In that moment, I forgot about the body lying by the bedroom doorway. The light from the hallway bathroom had been left on and it helped me see the rest of the room, although by then I pretty much knew my way around her place blindfolded. Her perfume, L'Air du Temps which normally seemed to hang in the air wherever she went, was just barely noticeable. Everything else in the room was pretty much the same with a few exceptions. The dresser by the door had been jostled and slightly moved out of place during the fight. Her queen size bed had a cream-colored duvet on it with two big pillows by the headboard. A small nightstand that normally stood beside it, however, had been knocked over in the struggle – or whatever you want to call it – and the Stephen King paperback as well as an old flip-number alarm clock radio was beside it on the floor. The other dresser, on the side of the room next to where I sat by the broken window, was intact and still housed the secrets of the diary she kept as a teenager. Right next to that she had a small desk with a computer and a picture of her old German Shepherd, Tartufo, who died when she was 17; that devastated her. A peach-colored trim against white walls usually gave the room a soft, warm feeling, but I couldn't find that warmth anymore. I think that the clouds had made it worse that night and everything just felt…different.

The alarm radio that was as lifeless as the body a few feet away had stopped at 8:54. I guessed it had broken during the fight. Through the ringing in my ears and the pounding headache that had come on suddenly, I heard the cops at the front door and that's when I knew it was all over. I looked up from the floor at the body again. Through the soft yellow light that spilled through the door, I was able to make out the bottom of the feet and I thought that the way they just laid there that night was…almost obscene.

When the cops finally got in, I couldn't move which was probably a good thing. I looked at her and thought about how beautiful she was. Maybe it was wrong of me to think that just then,

Chapter Two

I was a 30-year-old non-entity with a shy hairline, acid-reflux, and

% of my salary going into a 401K. I'd been working for about

r years in the customer service department at Astor House Books,

third largest bookstore chain in the country at the time. It was

job to talk to those hundreds of thousands of people crowding

bookstores across the country every day, slamming their money

n for cheap paperbacks and overpriced lattes. Before that, I was

ter. There's not much difference between the two, really. The

hing I'm thankful for is that at Astor House, I didn't have to

these people in the eye and smile while they complained that

eak was only medium-well and they had asked for well done.

the drawbacks to working at Astor House was that I didn't

quiet satisfaction of watching them relish the flavor of their

ell-done steak which, unknown to them of course, had only

ents before been laying under my shoe in the employee

right by the urinal.

ou're a Customer Service rep for a national bookstore

y other company for that matter, you spend your entire

I don't know. It really wasn't my intention for things to wi

way they did. And of course, I never meant to hurt her. I

done anything to keep her from any kind of hurt, which v

found myself in the position I was in that night. How th

come to that?

1(

fo

the

my

our

dow

a wa

only

look a

their st

One of

have th

newly w

just mon

bathroom

When

chain, or a

workday listening to the most inane complaints you could think of. You listen and then you apologize. You apologize because basically, that's what you're paid to do. I was paid to apologize. I apologized for seven hours a day, five days a week for things that weren't my fault.

Our department got calls from across the country. Everywhere there was a store. I got calls from California, Ohio, Florida, Arizona, even Hawaii. There wasn't a State that didn't have an Astor House Bookstore. That meant that anytime some red neck, socialite, or escaped mental patient with a grudge wanted to complain, I got to sit there and take it as long as they managed to weave Astor House Books into the plot. I once had a lady from Spokane, Washington take time out of her day to call our department to tell me that the water in the water fountain at the local store wasn't cold enough for her. She was really passionate in telling me just how important this was for her and how this "situation" (she actually called it a *situation*) was affecting her shopping experience. It was so troubling to her, in fact, that she was considering taking her business "elsewhere" where the fountains were "not too cold, but just cold enough – *Spokane* cold." She had already discussed this with the staff at the store but, apparently, no one there could do anything to help the *situation*. Naturally, they referred her to the corporate office. Of course, I apologized and told her that I would make sure our facilities department reviewed the water temperature at that location.

When you hear the word "department," you tend to think of a complex office set-up with a lot of people running around cubicles with papers and files in their hands; trying to make sure the whole damn world doesn't fall out from under them before five o'clock. In reality, our department consisted of four people, including me. Sofia Kanning worked in the cubicle next to mine. She was 38, short, anorexic and had just filed for divorce. Her flat, stringy blonde hair looked like someone took some angel hair pasta out of the pot, put it on her head and tried to manage it with a clip. Her clothes always seemed like they were too big for her and hung loosely like they were still on the hanger.

Brian Colworth was 25, had never worked retail before, but had a bachelor's in psychology, which somehow impressed the folks in human resources. Brian was also short, but stocky and his cubicle was right across from mine so I always got to see his face react to every call that he answered. Sometimes, he would throw his hands in the air or rub his eyes with the palms of his hands so hard that you would think he was trying to push them into his head.

The head of customer service, and my boss obviously, was George Marvel. I swear that's his name. Mr. Marvel. Even after four years, I couldn't bring myself to call him that. I usually just called him George. Mr. Marvel. That sounds like he should be wearing a cape with some sort of meaningful symbol on his chest, bringing hope to the citizens of Astorland and striking fear in the hearts of the nefarious ne'er-do-wells that try to infiltrate our beloved micropolis. George sat in a corner office facing our cubes and spent a majority of the time pulling reports, talking on the phone and criticizing us for not "sounding more sympathetic to the customer." He was in his forties, very muscular, black, married to a white woman, and had two kids who shared table space in a frame on his desk.

My last call that day, the day I first saw her, was from a guy in Cedar Rapids, Iowa complaining about the overhead music we had in our stores. "It's too damn loud. You can't concentrate on what you're reading. How the hell am I supposed to find what I'm looking for when I've got that God-awful sound blaring at me from the ceiling?!" Apology. "And it's not even music! It's some...some garbage that I've never heard of before." Justin Beiber. Apology. "Well, if you don't change it, I'll take my business elsewhere." I assured him that the *situation* would be taken care of.

The corporate office is located in downtown Manhattan, not too far from Wall Street. After work, I always heard people in the elevator talk about the bars they were planning to hit for happy hour. *Happy* hour. It's what some of these people live for. A chance to loosen the tie, get relatively smashed and build up the courage to mouth off about people you didn't like at the office or gripe about the unreasonable expectations from your supervisor. Sounds real happy. They had stopped asking me to join them years ago. I guessed it was because I never took them up on their offer. If I didn't like them while I was sober, I can only imagine how I would have reacted to them if I were drunk.

The walk to the train station was less than ten minutes. The ride home to Queens itself, was about forty, but it always took longer "due to a red signal ahead," or those people who couldn't wait for the next train and so they made a dive for the car and stopped the doors from closing. That's quite possibly the best form of torture I know of, having to ride with some of the people that called my office because they objected to our stores selling *Maxim* magazine (they considered it pornography). So, for a minimum of forty minutes, the enemy surrounded me.

Usually, they were involved in some kind of stupid effort to tune out the rest of the world. For example, that day there was this fat woman in a navy blue dress wedged up against me on the right, talking to her spectacled waif of a friend who sat in front of her, clutching her imitation Gucci handbag like everyone in the subway was eyeing it. "No, but I told her. I told her. I said 'Jaime, I don't know why you're still with him. He never seems to pay attention to you unless he needs money.'"

"You said that?"

"Oh, yeah."

"And what did she say?"

"Oh, well she nodded and told me that I was right. She said that she was going to leave him this weekend, but I think she's full of it. She doesn't have the guts to do something like that." You can't help but wonder what other sage advice she's capable of dispensing. It must be nice to have that kind of grasp on relationships that you're not involved in. I remember wishing she'd get a better grasp on the overhead bar so that she wouldn't bump into me every time the train moved.

Others sat there, nose buried deep in the book or magazine they brought to occupy their time during the commute. You'll hear countless numbers of languages engaged in conversation. Some recognizable, some from places most have never heard of, and still others trying so desperately to adapt to the American way of life, they left their first language waiting at home while they tried to get through the day with their adopted one. Some of them would just stare off into space, not looking at anything in particular, despite all the entertaining colorful propaganda by the doors. "Earn your degree in six months," "Give to charity, just not here," "H.I.V. changed my life." The more daring would sneak glances at other passengers, wondering what they're reading, thinking, talking about, or wearing underneath their clothes; quickly darting their eyes away when they'd get caught and tried to make it seem as if they were just looking around. I would be trapped in there with each of their fantasies, judgments, frustrations, and sweat. At least the phone at work kept me at a distance. During the winter, you could smell the wet wool as they stood next to you and the snow slowly melted into the different layers of their clothes. In the summer, body odors that you never thought possible attacked you and between the screech of the rails and the smell and the empty looks, before you knew it, you were in sensory overload.

It wasn't until the last stop in Manhattan where I started to feel better. First of all, most of the people on the car got off. Second, and more importantly, that's when she got on.

I had never seen her before. She wasn't wearing a wedding ring, but that stopped meaning something long ago. She got on at the 59th and Lexington Avenue stop. I managed to get a seat and noticed her walk by me and while she sat just a few feet away. She was tall, at least 5'9". Her short blonde hair seemed unaffected by whatever she had faced during the day. She wore nude heels and stockings, a tan skirt that just reached her knees, a white silk blouse that she had stopped buttoning at the fourth one up from the bottom and covered it with a tan blazer which matched the skirt. Her hands were milk white, while her cheeks had been slightly touched with a light blush; nothing that stood out too much, just enough that added a little color. In my opinion, she didn't need it. Her eyes were covered with a rather large pair of outdated Ray Ban Wayfarer sunglasses. She had the kind of frame that matched her height, a larger body, but not fat by any means.

I worked late that day and so I didn't get to the station at my usual time. After my last call, George had wanted me to draft a letter to a customer who had written to complain about the lighting in one of our stores in Maine. Apparently, it wasn't bright enough for his purposes. It took me four drafts before Captain Corporate

found the one he felt most appropriately conveyed the company's

sympathetic approach to his plight. I was drained and pissed off

when I got to the station at twenty to six and just barely missed

getting crushed by the closing doors. By the time we reached 59th

and Lexington, I was so upset over the whole ordeal, I started

entertaining my usual scenarios - where I'd go into the office and

answered my first call by telling the customer that they could go

fuck themselves if they didn't like our goddamn policy. George

would come out and ask me to repeat what I had just said. I'd stand

up and back him into his office where I would proceed to shout what

it was that I had told the customer. He'd ask me to calm down and

would remind me that we were there to serve our customers and to

make sure that they kept coming back to the stores. I'd respond by

pushing him out the window.

Anyway, as I sat there and smirked at the thought, she had

walked in and sat down. Of course, I wasn't the only one who

noticed her. The men she moved passed kept their eyes fixated on

her ass while she walked toward the seat. Those slimy bastards started to savagely undress her and lick their lips at the thought of what they would do to her if they had the chance. These were the kinds of guys who tried to look up the skirts at the women ahead of them on the escalators. I immediately hated that they were looking at her. She just ignored them, however, and discreetly sat down, casually turning the pages of her latest J. Crew catalog.

One stop and a borough later, we had emerged from the tunnel and were speeding toward the next station. When I realized that I had been staring at her, I tried to focus on the newspaper I had bought that morning, even though the news it detailed was, by 6:20, no longer *news*. She kept her hands and catalog in her lap as she looked over every piece of information about the random items on the pages. I noticed there was one too-young-to-remember-Clinton, red-power-tie-wearing bastard that sat directly across from her, who tried to smile at her when she looked up to check on the stop. Naturally, she didn't respond. In fact, she seemed not to notice him at all, which disturbed him enough for him to make his disappointment obvious in the tiny furrow of his perfectly straight eyebrows. He quickly looked down to try to disguise the rejection stamp so clearly marked on his square-jawed face, but it was too late. I had already seen it and it was beautiful.

She got off on Astoria Boulevard, the stop just before mine, Ditmars Boulevard. I tried not to make it too obvious as I was watched every move she made so I could commit every inch of her to memory, but I think that she had caught me. Her sunglasses kept her eyes covered, but I distinctly saw when she moved her face in my direction and held me like that for half a second before she gathered her purse to get off. Before I knew it, I had stood up, and watched her walk down the platform toward the stairs. When the doors closed behind her I found myself pressed against the window, vainly, as I tried to keep her in my sight for as long as possible before we pulled away. Unfortunately, other people had begun to crowd the platform behind her and soon she had disappeared in the cattle mass of gray, blue, and brown jackets moving toward the staircase. The train jerked once, as if to shake me from a dream and then started to roll to its final stop. I closed my eyes and tried to picture her face.

I don't even remember when the train pulled into Ditmars. The conductor's warped voice came through the overhead speakers and when I opened my eyes, I realized that I needed to use the opposite doors in order to get out. I kept thinking about her as I walked to the station exit, down the stairs, past the McDonald's with the homeless guy in front, and to my bus stop in front of Pizza Palace. She had looked at me just before she got off. At least, I thought she had. Maybe I had imagined it. Had I imagined it? Possibly.

Chapter Three

The bus I took, the Q19A, probably had the saddest route in Queens. It traveled through most of Astoria, which was basically divided into two extreme parts. There was the part that was east of 21st Street, which was like a Greek version of a Norman Rockwell painting. Nice neighborhoods, a mix of apartment buildings and three family houses with yards. Then there was the part that was west of 21st, which was referred to as Ravenswood. It was the type of neighborhood that was made to accommodate low-income families. In other words, it was the kind of place that you generally tried to avoid. It was a succession of conjoined buildings that stretched on block after block until you reached Shore Boulevard, which was then littered with various industrial warehouses. After that, the neighborhood dumped into the East River. On any given day, you could witness a mugging, a drive-by, or a gang initiation rite. Most of the time, though, all you'd see are drunks, drug addicts and hookers. On special occasions, you'd get a taste of all three rolled into one with a drunken, crack-head prostitute named Simone. Ravenswood, home.

The bus left me right on the corner of my block. The courtyard that served as the entrance to five identical gray buildings was usually peppered with small pieces of garbage and various tenants. I didn't know many of them and I didn't want to. For the most part, if you kept your head down and your mouth shut, you were safe. When I got to the lobby of my building, some Black and Hispanic kids were hanging out by a doorway next to the mailboxes. Simone's apartment. They were speaking some language which I'm sure was once English. It had been raped and broken and made into something distinctly theirs. They jostled one another and laughed when one of them made a reference to one of their own that was apparently in with her. They seemed to be waiting their turn. I walked past them and went right for the elevator without stopping to get my mail or looking directly at any of them.

My apartment was on the third floor at the end of a hallway walled with stains and torn vinyl tile. I always made sure to snap all three locks into place once I got in. I wouldn't touch the door again until morning. My nights were blessed with microwavable dinners and diet Pepsi. It was a little different that night, however. Instead of just settling down in front of the TV to eat and zone out until it was time to go to bed, I began to wonder what she was doing at that moment. Even though I had never seen her on the train before, there was something…familiar about her. I couldn't place it at the time, but there was something there that just reached out to me. She hardly struck me as the type that walked into an empty apartment. I doubted that the curry/steamed vegetables/bean and fart smells that welcomed me home every night was the kind of greeting that she got. I doubted that she ever saw a group of teenagers that waited to get their kicks with a middle- aged hooker on drugs. Whenever she looked out her window, she probably had a view of Astoria Park or maybe the Manhattan skyline. All I saw when I looked out my window were the apartments across the courtyard. That's why I kept the shades drawn.

At night the silence in my apartment let you listen to all the different lives around it. Sometimes, it was better than TV. Downstairs, for example, Mrs. Lopez would usually be yelling at her "no good son" and telling him, once again, that he "would never amount to anything." Next door, the Harrisons were usually watching some sort of action movie and would have the volume up so loud that I would hear all the cheesy dialogue in my room. The Walkers in the apartment above mine could always be counted on to have another marital spat where they ended each insult with a slamming door. On some nights, you could also hear the rap music in the courtyard crawling up to every apartment in the complex. Occasionally, the sound of an approaching siren would overwhelm all of them.

I found it hard to sleep that night. Usually, after I watched some TV, I'd go to bed and eventually drift off. That night, though, I couldn't help but review the day I'd had. Everything from work to the moment I saw her on the train. She was incredible. Of course I felt kind of stupid thinking so much about a woman I hadn't even met, but still, I knew then that she was different from everyone else. I could tell just by the way she carried herself. She didn't slouch; she looked well groomed and was stylishly dressed. Her shoes didn't have a scuffmark on them. You could tell that she was some sort of professional. I started to wonder if maybe she was in the health care industry or worked with some sort of children's services.

Just by the way that she rejected that metrosexual idiot on the train told me that she was probably a very kind person. She was probably not even able to say a harsh word to anyone. I knew that she had seen me. She probably thought that I was just like all the other guys that stared at her. That was the last thing I wanted her to think. She was beautiful and clean in the middle of all that filth that surrounded her and she probably thought of me as one of them. Just another pair of eyes that roamed over her; another pair to ignore.

Chapter Four

When the train pulled into the Astoria Boulevard station the next morning, I put my newspaper down and looked at everyone getting on, with the hopes that I would see her. I deliberately rode on the same car I had ridden the day before - fourth from the front - and I watched the blur of people speed by as we slowed down. I thought I had caught a glimpse of blonde hair, but it turned out to be a guy. When I realized that she wasn't getting on, I slumped back against my seat as the doors closed. Rather than go on reading my paper, I just folded it in half and stared at the floor for the rest of ride.

There was a red signal, so I got to work about five minutes late. After I apologized to George, I sat down, switched on my computer and put on the headset. The first call I got was from a lady in Ohio who was calling from her cell phone on her way to work. She wanted to let us know about the wonderful service she received from one of our B.A.s. "Oh Missy was sooo helpful yesterday. I walked into your store and I needed to buy a gift for my neighbor's little boy and I just didn't know what to get. I mean, the boy's only five years old and I don't have any children so I had absolutely no idea what to buy. So I thought, I'll go to Astor House."

For calls like this, there was an entirely different approach. The same amount of patience was needed, but you had to handle it differently. After you got over the unsettling feeling of someone being that sickeningly sweet that early, you had to send an e-mail to the Region Manager in charge of that store, with a "cc" to the Store Manager. First, though, you had to send it to George so he could approve the e-mail before you sent it. Never mind that we had a "form template" of such an e-mail already saved in the computer that we used every time we got one of these calls, he still wanted to see it to make sure that we were "dotting all the i's and crossing all the t's". After his "Okay", you sent the e-mail, "cc-ing" him as well so that the Region Manager saw that you communicated everything through George.

The phones started to ring before we even got to the office. Customers left messages on our voice mail system and Brian was in charge of listening to all of them (one of the drawbacks of getting the early shift) and then he gave them to George so that he could slice up the calls evenly between us. There weren't that many messages that day. Normally we got anywhere from eight to twelve. I came in early once and heard Brian talking back to the messages. All that pent up frustration of never being able to say what you wanted for the whole day just burst out at each of the customers who felt compelled to let us know about some shocking new outrage that could dissuade them from shopping with us again. I never let him know that I had heard him. Brian was in rare form. He was hurling insults and damnations on every faceless voice he heard; mocking them, imitating them. It was the first time in years that I smiled before starting work.

After I got George's approval to send Missy's Store Manager and Region Manager an e-mail complimenting her customer service skills, I went to the break room to get some coffee. The break room is on the other side of the floor, so I had to pass through other departments and listen to the kind of day they were having. I wasn't even sure what half of those people did or even knew exactly what department they were in. All I saw were a bunch of people that hung around each other's cubes and talked on the phone or were in their supervisor's office (the same one they'd trash later at "happy hour"). In some cubes, you'd sometimes saw someone hard at work while they stared at the monitor and furiously tapped away at the keyboard. Everyone was involved in their own project. Even the ones that traded office gossip and gave you a polite but ineffectual smile or the insincere, "How ya doin'?" as you walked by were involved in their own project. Customer Service is the only department that never had any time for this sort of p.c. socialization. Not that I'm complaining. I didn't want to be involved in that bullshit.

On my way back from the break room, Floyd Wallace bumped into me as he walked out of his cube. Floyd was usually in a perpetual rush. He worked in our Risk Management department. They were the guys that dealt with every accident that happened in the stores. If someone slipped on some wet tile in the bathroom, they got the accident report, contacted our insurance company, and filed the case. He was kind of a nervous guy, rail thin and had thick, coke-bottle glasses. For some reason, he always looked wet. His greasy, dark hair was always getting in his eyes and you could generally find him apologizing to someone in the hallway for bumping into them. He started in the mailroom and worked his way out. He ate lunch alone, always a tuna fish sandwich on white, which he brought from home wrapped in aluminum foil. Floyd liked to go to lunch late, usually around 2 or so. He did this so as to avoid seeing anyone in the break room since most everyone else went anywhere between Noon and 1. You could always find him sitting at the same table in the farthest corner of the room, reading a newspaper and never looking up unless you said his name.

"Sssorry. I...I'm sorry. Sorry." He adjusted the loose frame on his face and clutched the folders in his arms closer to his chest. His tie, naturally, was crooked and hung just above his belly button. "Hi Floyd." It took him a second to realize who I was. I was one of the few people who actually had conversations with him.

"Oh...hel...hi, Everest. H-how are you?"

"Ok, thanks. How are you, Floyd?"

"Um...I'm...uh, I'm...good. Thanks. Just, uh, just going to make some...copies. How's it over in uh, in...Customer Service?"

"Same as always."

"Um…can't…you can't complain because…no one would listen, huh?" he smiled at his own joke, which he seemed to be telling his shoes. Floyd never looked anyone in the eyes. "That's right," I said, smiling. I think he noticed.

"Sssee you later." I watched him as he sped toward the end of the hall, sticking close to the wall until he turned the corner.

When I got back to my cube, I got a few calls from people objecting to some of the books in the stores. Sometimes it seemed as if they had a problem with every single book out there and I wondered if they'd be happy with all those shelves being occupied instead with hardcovers filled with blank, multi-colored pages. I began to wonder what kind of books she read. She didn't strike me as the lonely, frustrated, Harlequin romance type. And I doubted that she was the type to complain about anything that was being sold. Not her. If she saw something that she objected to, she probably just wouldn't even bother with it. I didn't think that she would call some company to try and force them to conform to whatever she felt was "acceptable" or call to point out what their "moral obligations" were.

My phone rang and the customer on the other end didn't even let me finish my greeting ("Astor House Customer Service, this is Everest. How may I help you?"). I got as far as "Astor House" before she cut me off to express her outrage that the stores were selling *Penthouse* magazine. In these scenarios, there wasn't not a lot that one could say other than the stores were going to comply with their request and would remove the titles that offended them. That was not going to happen, naturally, and so I let her drone, apologized and closed my eyes while she hurled a few curses at me before hanging up.

Sofia told me that the first time she got one of these calls, she cried for fifteen minutes after the person hung up on her. After a while, though, she would hang up on them once they started getting too loud. Not right away. First, she would tell them to "lower" their voices. The second time they started to yell, they got disconnected. Even after all this time, it took a lot for me to hang up on someone. Despite whatever unreasonable demand they were making, I still couldn't bring myself to do it. I think it's rude. Besides, most times, they would just wind up calling back and we would have to deal with them anyway. At least with me, they got to speak (or yell) their minds and then we'd be done with them. Off to build their web campaign against the big, fat, greedy corporation and its various heads that get blind, stinking rich strictly off the sale of pornography and frappucinos.

The next few calls I had that led up to lunch weren't anything major. A few questions about our return policy, some old lady who complained that there were too many books by foreigners in our stores, and one guy who called to say that he would like to see Astor House set up a bookstore somewhere out in Buttsville, IA. Lunch for me usually consisted of fast-food and *The Daily News*. As soon as I got settled, I'd go straight for the comic section. After a few mouthfuls of pizza or some other artery-clogging morsel, I would go back to the beginning of the paper and worked my way to sports. A few disappointing articles on the Mets and I was out with twenty-five minutes to spare.

There was a store just a few blocks away from the office and sometimes, I would stand in front and watched as the crowds went by. Everybody was immersed in their own little world and they didn't even notice someone like me sizing them up and matching them to the million different voices that I've talked to across the country. I had gotten to the point where I stopped seeing people as individuals and just viewed them as complaints; whiney, pedantic complaints. As I watched them file in and out of the store, I wondered what she did for lunch. At first, going by the way she was so nicely dressed, I guessed that she probably ate out in a real restaurant with some coworkers. But then, I thought that the way she carried herself when she walked by me, she probably just brought a simple sandwich in to work. Seeing as how she got on the train at 59th Street, she obviously worked in midtown. There was an Astor House store around that area as well. I remember thinking what a shame it was that the office wasn't located there. Then maybe, I would have been able to have seen her around lunch. Maybe, if her job were close enough, she went to the store during her lunch hour and then I definitely would have been able to see her.

Instead, I got to watch some homeless guy slumped up against the building, holding a sign that asked people for money.

There were only a couple of voice mails when I got back to the office. Anytime somebody went on break, we had to check the voice mail system for any calls that may have been missed by the other two service reps. Most times, on hearing an automated message as opposed to a live person, the customer got more aggravated and their frustration would come out in an obnoxious, singsong type of tone. "Well, your message says that you're open from 8 am to 6 pm Eastern Standard Time and it's only 12:30 pm so why isn't anyone answering the phone?!" Really made you want to call back.

The rest of the afternoon went by smoothly enough. George was in an afternoon meeting, so I actually left on time. It wasn't until I got to the train station that I realized that I should wait before getting on the train. After all, I had gotten out late the day I saw her so maybe that's the time she got out of work. Then again, maybe she had been held up like I was and that's why she wound up getting to the station at that hour.

Summer in Manhattan meant that you'll lose about eight pounds in water weight while you waited for a train to come. Everything bothers you when you're hot and stuck in a tunnel. The foot long black rats that scurried around the rails for example, or the banshee-like screech of every train that pulled into the station. If those didn't do it, then the other passengers would definitely irritate you. What made it worse was that you couldn't do anything about it. Rather than take the chance and wait, I decided to just hop on the first N train that came by.

There was a young emo couple making out on the seat in the corner reserved for handicapped people, everybody else was reading. While I watched the local stops spin past me, I started to wonder what she'd be wearing. A black suit. Maybe a string of pearls. Of course, I couldn't picture her without the sunglasses as well. I remembered that I started to get angry when I pictured everyone staring at her, letting their imagination roam over her body; touching, tasting, grabbing, sliding. Each and every set of new hands seeking to satisfy some sick desire.

When the stop finally came, I tried not to make it too obvious that I was looking for her. My eyes darted from one blank, stale face to the next. People crowded in, indiscreetly trying not to notice that their butts were rubbing against each other. Nothing. Somebody called out, "Could ya move a lil' further in please?!" Still nothing. A short lady who was trying to keep her distance from some guy's armpit answered, "Where you want us to go?" The doors were having trouble closing because the crowd was keeping them apart. I thought that she could very well be on the platform, but couldn't get through because of the crowd. As I got up from my seat, I managed to squeeze between the small spaces in-between everyone, but I couldn't get through to the door. "Excuse me, ma'am," I said. The old lady I was pressed up against just sneered at me. Finally, the doors closed and a moment later, we were moving into the tunnel.

At the next stop, Queensboro Plaza, I got off with everybody else and waited on the platform. I figured that she had to be on the next train. It was roughly the same time that it had been when I saw her. My train finally pulled away and like every one else who got to the station, I leaned over the tracks to see if there was another one coming. From where I was standing, I could see most of Astoria sprawled out in front of me. I saw pieces of Ravenswood peeking out behind warehouses and decent apartment buildings that never heard of Simone or saw the gang colors hanging out of the back pockets of jeans that rode well below some kid's waist. I saw the Triborough Bridge in the distance, lanes crowded in a mad panic of rush hour traffic. Everybody's got somewhere to go, someplace they wanted to get to and vegetate. The sooner they'd get home, the sooner they could eat, the sooner they could see which set of celebrities won the next round of "Dancing with the Stars."

Leaning over the tracks again, I thought about the lying bastard conductor who said that there was "another train *right behind* this one." Finally, I heard the familiar shriek of a train in the distance. My palms started to sweat. Would she be on it? Would she be alone? I kept wondering. The shriek was getting closer. I leaned over a little more, but I still couldn't see anything. More and more people began to gather on the platform, empty faces sporting that dull, tired look in the eyes. Just below the station, I could see the pink and blue neon sign for *Jiggles*, a new topless bar which boasted

of having "the hottest girls on the East Coast." Somebody bumped

into me and didn't bother to say, "Excuse me." When I looked down

the platform, I saw the 7-train shriek to a stop on the other side of the

platform. "Right behind" must have meant something else to that

guy.

Five full minutes later, the doors to the front car of the N stopped

right in front of me. I let everybody out and casually walked inside.

I wanted to sit in the same seat I had yesterday, but some big fat guy

with a *Yankees* cap was already sitting there, napping while some

drool escaped from the corner of his mouth. Walking over to the

doors next to him, I stood for the rest of the trip. The fat guy stirred

a little, briefly closed his mouth and then let it drop open again once

the train rocked him back to sleep.

Right in middle of the car, I saw her sitting in the same place

looking through a Disney catalog instead. That day, she wore a navy

blue, pinstriped pantsuit that revealed a gold cross hanging from a

thin gold chain around her neck. She still had the sunglasses on.

Her navy blue high heels looked like they had just been taken out of the box. This time, there weren't any meat bags in a suit eyeing her from his seat. There was no whiny, pretty-boy jerk-off with pliable paste-covered hair sending out "the vibe." Everyone seemed to be minding their own business for once. The only sound was the running of the tracks. It became a steady, almost melodic noise.

People got off and on and she never once looked up. This one woman took out her cell phone and began loudly discussing what her plans were for the night. "Nah, I'm at 36th right now. Uh-huh. Uh-huh. Right. Well why don't you…listen girl, why don't you just go to Rueben's house? Will you listen for a sec? Look…I know, but…just, just go to his house and I'll be there in a little while. I'll change my clothes and we'll go to that bar on 45th and 30th. You know the one that he always goes to. We'll probably bump into him and that bitch there. Uh-huh. So?! We'll catch them by surprise. You know the place, right? Some Irish bar, I don't know what it's called. Yeah, it's right on the corner. Uh-huh. Yeah. Ok. Ok. Nah, don't even worry about it. Shit, it's the least I can do. Ok girl, I'll see you in a while. Right. Ok. Lay-tah." She put the phone back in her purse and shot me a dirty look before going back to reading *The Seven Spiritual Laws of Success*. Even the fat guy next to me had woken up when she started talking. But not her. She just kept flipped through her catalog as if nothing could shake her concentration. She didn't even have that annoying habit of licking her fingers before turning the page, either. Every move was natural and fluid. I remember wishing to just see her eyes, just once. I just wanted to watch them glide across the page and see what sparked an interest.

Just before we got to Astoria Boulevard, the door at the end of the car slid open and Ben walked through. Ben was an older homeless man with a withered left hand and a graying beard. Summer, winter, or fall, he was always bundled up in the same clothes and the smell that clung to him was a mixture of sour milk and old cigarettes. Ben's shtick was that he would say if you couldn't give him any money, he'd take a smile. Most people didn't even give him that much. "Good evening ladies and gentlemen, my name is Ben. I am a homeless man and I apologize for interrupting your ride. I'm trying to do the best I can with what I got, but I still need your help if you can spare it. If you don't have any change, please just give me a smile." He started to walk through the car but nobody bothered to look up at the guy. When he got to her, not only did she look up and smile, but she took out a sandwich in a plastic Ziploc out of her bag and gave it to him. Ben smiled back and blessed her. She went back to looking at the Mickey Mouse-inspired merchandise.

Ben tucked the sandwich into a stretched out, black coat pocket and he moved down the car in the hopes that maybe he'd get some sort of similar kindness from someone else. No such luck, though. No one else even acknowledged his presence. They had all perked up their ears when that loudmouth was talking on the phone, but no one could be bothered to give Ben so much as a casual glance when he walked past them - except her. When he got to me, I had managed to fish out all the change I had left, which amounted to .37. He thanked me, walked to the front of the car and stared out the door window. She put the catalog in her tote bag.

When the train pulled into Astoria Boulevard, she got her things together and left, along with everyone else, including Ben. I didn't get a look that time, though, she just walked out. Instantly, I wondered if that was on purpose. Maybe since she had caught me looking at her last time and was deliberately avoiding looking in my direction so as not to encourage me? I didn't want to think about it. Without realizing it, I stood up and walked over to where she sat moments before. The train had already pulled out and was stopped between stations. How much time had passed? Seconds? Minutes? As I stood there with my eyes closed, I sniffed the air and I swear that I found a trace of her perfume. It was only just barely noticeable so I leaned in closer, inches from where she had been and inhaled deeply, desperately trying to draw as much of it in as possible. There was something very familiar about the scent, but I couldn't place it at the time. When it started to fade, I felt as if something in my head was trying to grab hold of a memory, something lost and buried somewhere through the haze of the years. I stayed perfectly still, afraid to move and lose it. The last thing I wanted was to disrupt that moment. I would've given anything to wrap myself up in that scent, to rediscover whatever it was I was trying to recall. When I finally exhaled, I couldn't wait to draw in another breath. I know it sounds crazy but it almost felt like I could have brought her closer to me if I could have held onto that scent. It was so familiar, almost comforting...warm. She smiled at me in that aftermath, that after-image she left behind, her head tilted coyly.

"Ditmars Boulevard. Last Stop. Ditmars Boulevard, last stop on the N." The doors opened and I shot up just as a guy in a gray jogging suit walked in. Ignoring him, I rushed out and hurried down the stairs. On the bus ride home, I thought about how she smiled at Ben. Even though I couldn't see her eyes, I could tell that they smiled too. I think he appreciated that more than the sandwich. Well, maybe not. Still, I'm sure it was better than the faceless others that drop some coins into his cup and feel that they'd done their good deed for the day. She did it because she wanted to help him, not out of some false sense of moral obligation. I wondered where the sandwich came from. She probably had brought it for lunch like I had imagined earlier and for whatever reason, didn't eat it. Rather than throw it out, she probably held on to it just in case she would come across someone who was hungry. When the moment presented itself where it could do someone some immediate good, she gave it up without a second thought. She gave it to someone who genuinely needed some food. It was such a pure moment of

genuine kindness. I hadn't seen that in a long time.

Chapter Five

"I just want you to know right from the start that I spend hundreds of dollars at your stores every year. *Hundreds*. People like me are the reason your company stays in business. I just want to make that clear right from the get go. Got me?"

"Yes, ma'am."

"Good, long as that's understood."

"Yes, ma'am, I understand."

"Good. I find it deeply offensive and obnoxious that your stores don't offer free bookmarks to customers."

"I'm sorry, ma'am?"

"Bookmarks. I spend hundreds of dollars on books every year at your store and never once have I ever been given a free bookmark. I mean I know that you *sell* bookmarks. But why don't you give any away to your customers for free? I think that that's totally obnoxious and offensive. Furthermore, I think it's completely lacking in customer service."

This wasn't a service issue, she just wanted something for free. She wouldn't come right out and say it, but that's all she wanted.

The department got more of those kinds of "what are you gonna do to keep me as a customer?" calls than almost any other kind. It really had become a counter-thumper's world.

By 9:30 Brian was already on his fourth cup of coffee. Sofia called out sick so that meant that Brian and I had to bear the brunt of the calls and the e-mails that came in. In addition to the calls, we got an average of fifteen to twenty e-mails a day from customers with questions and issues as diverse as the calls. Brian usually handled the bulk of them, but George sifted through the Customer Service inbox and gave some to Sofia and me as well.

Lunchtime finally arrived and as I was halfway done with my slice, I happened to glance at the entrance and for a second, I thought I saw her walk in. It turned out not to be her, though, so I took another bite and re-read the same sentence in the paper for the fifth time. I was having trouble concentrating on the article. My mind kept wandering back to yesterday and how she helped Ben and of course, that perfume that I still couldn't place but couldn't forget.

"H…Hi Everest. Mind if I uh, if I sit with you?" Floyd materialized at my side, holding a tray with a slice and a fountain soda.

"No, not at all, Floyd. Please sit." He half smirked and sat down in front of me. The table tipped toward him and his drink almost slid off the edge. We both managed to stop it in time and steadied the makeshift seesaw. "So, Floyd, what's brings you here? I don't think I've ever seen you eat lunch at this hour, especially outside the break room. What happened to your sandwich?"

"Oh, I uh…I ffforgot it. Ha-ha. Can you imagine? I made it this morning and then left it on the counter. Huh."

"Well, that happens."

"An…and the train made me late this morning, so I couldn't buy my uh, my…breakfast and newspaper on the way in. Didn't have time. So I thought I'd…um, have lunch early. So hungry," he smiled.

Normally, I preferred to eat lunch on my own but I didn't mind Floyd. He was okay. "How're things in customer service?"

"Pretty much the same. How're they treating you in Risk Management?"

"Um…they're…they're ok. I got…an interesting case," he blushed.

"Oh yeah? What happened?"

"Um…well there's this lady out in, um, in Phoenix who had an accident in our store." He took another bite of his slice and quickly glanced around to see if anyone from the office was around. "She uh, she…slipped in the bathroom."

"What's so interesting about that?"

"She…she was having sex with someone in the stall at the time."

I only stopped for a second. I had actually heard of it before. Not that specific instance, but others like it. Floyd was smiling and snickering at the table. "Let me guess, she's suing the company?" I asked. It wouldn't have surprised me in the least. Even if you caught them with their pants down and their dicks in between the pages of *The Symposium*, they'd still give you that "what'd I do?" look and try to sue. "How'd you know?" he asked.

"I would have been surprised if you had said that she wasn't." I finished my slice, but I felt bad for wanting to leave so I stuck around. We didn't say much to each other. Floyd was too focused on that pizza. "You ever get…tired?" I asked.

"Hmm?"

"I mean, you deal with virtually the same type of people that I deal with. Albeit in different circumstances, but occasionally, you get somebody like this woman who's suing the company now because she slipped on some wet tile while she was getting…having sex in the restroom. Does it bother you? I mean, when you were talking to her, did you just want to…you know…tell her--" I could tell he had no idea what I was talking about. He actually looked at me with those blank, doe-like eyes behind a pair of stupid binocular-type glasses and just blinked a couple of times. Of course he didn't know what I was talking about. He was just happy to have a job and eat his tuna sandwich when he didn't leave it on the counter. "Floyd," I said, not sure how to make a graceful exit, "I gotta go."

"Sssee you at the office, Everest."

After lunch, George called me into his office. "Have a seat, Everest." He was pretending to be really wrapped up in some papers that he was flipping through. It was all bullshit. George always did that when he called you into his office. It was his way of making you wait and wonder what you were "in trouble" for, it was a complete power trip. He wanted you to sweat and undermine yourself so that by the time he did open his goddamn mouth, you'd be so paranoid that you'd admit to the Kennedy assassination if he accused you of it. "Uh, Everest. I got a call from Joe Small's office while you were at lunch." Joe Small's office, more bullshit intimidation tactics. You were supposed to turn pale and shit your pants when you were told that the office of the president of Astor House Books called about something you did. It was Rita the Admin for God's sake. Joe was usually on the back nine. "Oh?"

"Yes. Do you remember a Harry Scott?" I got an average of twenty-five to thirty calls a day. And that's on a slow day. That's approximately 150 different names a week, all with different problems. Unless it was something that was totally off-the-wall, never-heard-before, it wasn't likely that I'd remember what this guy's damage was. Of course I didn't remember Harry Scott. If I had my choice, I wouldn't remember my own name. "Sorry George doesn't ring a bell."

"Well, he remembers you. Apparently, he called here and spoke to you about an order he placed at a store in Miami. *Flights of Fancy: America's First Contact with UFO's and What The Government*

Doesn't Want You to Know by Hamilton Gray. Sound familiar now?"

"Somewhat."

"Somewhat. Well, he placed an order for that book at the store two months ago and he still hadn't received it. As a matter of fact, he paid extra for an overnight delivery."

"I see."

"He wrote a letter to Joe saying that he spoke with you and that you promised to look into this but you never got back to him."

"Really?"

"Yes. I have a copy of the letter right here." He handed me the copy and while I still had no idea what this guy was referring to, I apologized to George and told him that I would look up his file in the computer. "I already did that," he said. "I found the file. On July 15th, you noted down that you had forwarded Mr. Scott's information to the special order department. That was a month ago."

"Ok."

"So, what happened?"

"Gee I…I don't know, George. It looks like special orders never called him."

"That's right, and neither did you."

"Well, I thought we were supposed to refer all customers with these kinds of inquiries to the special order department on Long Island so they could research it and call the customer with the status of their order."

"Yes, but you never called the customer to let him know that you had forwarded his information. So you see we're the ones to blame now even though special orders dropped the ball. They're saying that they never got this from you."

"George, I can pull up the e-mail and show you when I sent it to Marcy in their group."

"Not necessary. When I got this, I pulled up my own records and found the e-mail that you cc'd me on. It was dated July 15th, so we have that as a back up. We still look bad, though, because the customer was waiting to hear from you. You should've called him to let him know that you had forwarded his concerns and that Marcy from special orders would call him regarding his order. Then we'd be out of the loop, understand?"

"Yes, I do. I'm sorry."

"These are the kinds of mistakes that make us look bad, Everest. It makes us look like we're slacking off and I don't want anyone to ever get that impression from our group. You know better than this."

"Yes, George. I'm sorry. It won't happen again. I'll try my best."

"I hope it doesn't, Everest. I really, really hope that it doesn't. We work too hard for something like this to come back and bite us. Especially something like this that could be so easily avoided. This is something that somebody who just joined us would do. Rookie stuff, you know? You're no rookie. You forward a customer to another department, you contact them and let them know. Ok?"

Chapter Six

For some reason, when I got back to my desk I thought about what I saw her do on the train the day before. There she was, reaching into her bag to give a total stranger some food because he was obviously hungry. There was someone with a real problem and she didn't think twice about trying to help. And I had just been reprimanded because some guy had a tantrum over not getting a book about aliens. Suddenly, I felt sick and my grip on the armchair loosened a little. Something in the pit of my stomach just didn't feel right. My hands were sweaty and I started to feel a stabbing headache come on. The phones were ringing and Brian picked up one of the calls. I rubbed my eyes and when I opened them, everything was blurry. I couldn't even pick up the next call that came in. Instead, I called out to Brian that I wasn't feeling well and ran to the bathroom.

Cold water. I ran the faucet and began to wet my face. I remember thinking, *"What the hell is wrong with me?"* or maybe I said it out loud. *"There you go. Just calm down."* I told myself that there was no need to get that upset. It was just some asshole, the same kind I'd been dealing with for five years. The water started to feel good. When I closed my eyes and instead of the usual off-color pink I saw in the mirror, I saw…her. Clear in my mind, she was standing somewhere in a field, smiling. So pure. There were no phones ringing, no mission statement index cards, no cubicles…it was as if the very thought of her pushed all that ugliness away. Instantly, I started to feel better and so I focused on her. She was wearing the same navy blue suit she had on the last time I saw her. I saw her so clearly it was like I was almost touching her. I couldn't even hear the faucet anymore. It was just her, the sky, the field and her scent. My face started to feel cool as I saw her walking towards me and I felt so much better. I saw the sun reflecting off her Ray Bans and her blonde hair was even more radiant than it had been on the train. Each step she took towards me made me feel better and better and I was able to smell her perfume again, it was like something out of a dream.

And then suddenly, it got cloudy and she stopped walking. I started to walk toward her, hoping not to lose that moment. That dream, or whatever it was, got darker with every step I took and I couldn't see her well. She had begun turning around and around, slowly spinning where she stood. The drops of water on my face were starting to bother me, like an annoying drizzle that won't let you see clearly. Out of nowhere, a wind kicked up and made her suit jacket flutter wildly. I struggled to reach her and noticed that she wasn't smiling anymore. As I got closer, the suit changed into a dark blue, ratty bathrobe and I felt a quick flash of anger go through me. My feet were sinking into the mud deeper and deeper with every step I took and yet, she just kept twirling slowly while the rain came down. When I finally reached her, the sky was completely dark and I was knee deep in the muddy ground. Reaching up, I grabbed her with both my arms and I realized that she wasn't spinning by herself. She was hanging from a branch with a noose around her neck and instead of sunglasses, her eyes were completely black.

That's when I felt the pizza come up.

When I got back to my cube, Brian had just hung up with a customer. "Jesus, man, are you ok?" he asked. My face was pale and still damp from all the water. I nodded at him and felt like I was going to get sick again when the phone rang. "What happened?" Brian asked, ignoring the phone.

"Nothing. I'm fine."

"Like hell you are. Do you know what you look like?"

"I...I don't..."

"Have a seat, man. Do you want some water or something?"

"No. No more water, thanks."

"What's going on?" George came out of his office, wondering why no one bothered to answer the last call. He actually stopped short when he saw me. "What's the matter, Everest?"

"Nothing, I'm fine. Just a little queasy."

"He ran to the bathroom before and came back like this," Brian explained.

"You throw up?" George asked, keeping his eyebrows knit.

"No. A little. Just a little. Bad pizza."

"Maybe you should go home," Brian said.

"Maybe I should make that call," George shot back. "You wanna go home, Everest?"

George hated to let anyone go early. You could have a tumor the size of a bowling ball growing out of your neck and it wouldn't make any difference to George. Captain Corporate. Mr. Sensitivity.

Of course, I took advantage of the opportunity and told George that I'd like to go home. He nodded and as he walked back to his office, he tossed a casual, "Hope you feel better" over his shoulder at me. The whole time I spent getting from the office to Astoria was a blur. I was aware of the people around me, the sights and sounds, but none of it seemed real. Whatever the hell it was that happened to me in the bathroom, suddenly made me remember what had struck me so much about her perfume. It was L'Air du Temps, the same kind my mother wore.

We lived in the Williamsburg section of Brooklyn, my mother and I, before it became trendy to do so. My father left when I was 5 and I never heard from him again. Unfortunately, my mother never really got over it. She sunk into a deep depression, became a raging alcoholic, and lost a few jobs before she wound up working in a dress factory on Kent Avenue. Needless to say, we didn't have much. Except for company, of course, the male kind. My mom had plenty of those, sometimes more than one at a time. I guess it was understandable; she was really beautiful and men were just really attracted to her. She had this curly blonde hair that fell just past her shoulders. I remember that she had a really kind smile, those few times I actually saw it. When she did, though, it had a way of making you feel better. She was slender, but had these curvy legs that she liked to show off in short skirts. I was never mistreated or abused by her, but I never felt like I was her first priority. Some of the men she brought home were nice; most of them ignored me. Her drinking got better when she first started dating them, but once they left, she slid back to being drunk most of the time.

One thing they all did, no matter how long they were together, was eventually get her a bottle of her favorite perfume, L'Air du Temps. She'd wear it often, most of the time when she was going out on a date. Sometimes, during her more sober moments, she'd take me to the park or if she had managed to save enough money, to the movies. I didn't have many friends growing up, so I always looked forward to spending time with her. The nights when she would pass out on the couch in front of the TV with an empty glass in her hand were the nights I most worried about her. I would sit there, stroke her hair and just stare at her, hoping that she'd wake up. No matter how many times I tried to wake her, she would just turn over and keep snoring. Sooner or later, I'd wind up asleep on the floor next to her.

I had just gotten home from school that afternoon when I found her. I was twelve and had made the honor role for the first time in my life. As soon as the bell rang, I grabbed my schoolbag and ran the eight blocks home, my report card and honor roll certificate in my hand. I remember racing up the stairs and hoping that she hadn't already started drinking. After fishing my keys out of my pocket, I fumbled with the three locks on the door before finally getting inside. The apartment was dark when I walked in and I wondered at first if she was even home. She had lost her job at the factory a few days before that and had been binge drinking since, so I thought that maybe she had gone out to buy more booze. I felt this lump of disappointment in the pit of my stomach as I went from room to room in that tiny apartment, calling out her name but not seeing her anywhere. I did, however, find an opened eviction notice on the small coffee table we had by the couch. As I sat on the edge of my bed, looking at my honor roll certificate, it suddenly didn't seem that important anymore.

That's when I noticed the light coming from the under the bathroom door. I thought that maybe she just hadn't heard me calling her, and would come out soon. Mentally, I started psyching myself up by thinking how happy this news would make her. After about fifteen minutes, though, I walked over and lightly tapped on the door. There had been times when I'd come home from school and she'd be in the bathroom sick from all that she drank, but it seemed so quiet in there. Knocking again a little harder, I called out to her but still didn't hear anything. After waiting a few more minutes, I knocked again, but still didn't get an answer. I pressed my ear to the door, and tried to listen for any kind of movement or maybe even snoring (she had passed out in the bathroom once or twice), but there was nothing. Finally, I tried the doorknob and opened the door.

The very first thing I noticed, for some reason, was that she had painted her toes. I knew that she had painted them and hadn't gone to get a pedicure because she had gotten some of the bright red nail polish on her actual toes as well as the nails. They stood out in contrast against the white tub, which she seemed to float over. She was wearing her old blue bathrobe, tied at the waist. Her face had changed color and I had thought that she was wearing make-up at first. Standing frozen in the doorway, I felt my certificate fall out of my hand as I noticed that her head was tilted in a really unusual angle. And then I saw the brown extension cord that had been tied around her neck, leading up to the showerhead.

Later on, I was told there was a note. "I'm sorry." That was it. That's what she left behind to explain what she did. I remember throwing it away the day some distant cousin in Jersey came to take me to live with her.

When I got home, I shook the darkness of that memory away and managed to distract myself with some of the junk mail on top of my already paper-covered coffee/dining table. Despite the overpowering smell of various cuisines, my throat was still a little rough from throwing up earlier and so I opted not to eat and settled instead for a Heineken and some TV. Somewhere in the middle of the news, the phone rang but I let the machine get it. Of course, it was for Sanchez. "Sanchez, man, yo it's me bro, Emilio! Pick up the phone, man. Come awn, yo. Aight lissen. Me and Chulo's gonna be at Minerva's 'til 'bout…ten an' shit. Afta dat, we goin' ta Helix, cuz. Fuckin' come awn out, man. What the fuck, bro, you go and disappear an' shit. Aight, laytah." I had been getting those messages for about a week. Of course I could have answered it and let this idiot know that he had the wrong number, but after answering the phones at work, the last thing I wanted to do was pick up another stupid call.

Chapter Seven

I did some necessary food shopping Saturday morning and after I stared at the wall for twenty minutes, I got up and took the bus to Steinway Street. The bus left me a block away from the Astoria Museum of the Moving Image, where they had a feature on silent movies. Chaplin, Valentino, Keaton, they were all there with a few behind the scene tidbits. It's an odd feeling when you watch those movies. You know what the sounds are, but there's no Dolby Digital system surrounding you to confirm what you hear echoing in your head. No explosions or predictable cheesy lines. There's just this constant silence amid all the chaos that keeps you distant from the actual movie. Everyone else in the theater was older than me with the exception of two film students periodically jotting something down in a notebook for future dissection.

Two hours later I was outside again and lunch came in the form of a souvlaki stick and a Pepsi I bought from a vendor near the Baby Gap store on the corner. As I stood against the building, I started looking for her in that procession of nameless, faceless possibilities; each and every one a let down. It wasn't such a far out hope that I could see her in the crowd. She did, after all, seemed to live in Astoria and that's what most Astorians did on Saturday - shop on Steinway Street. Maybe my mistake was in thinking that she would be like most Astorians. She was probably at home, lounging on a sensible futon while catching up with the rest of the world in *The New York Times*, a half empty espresso cup resting next to her on a glass end table. Maybe her phone would ring and it would be one of her friends, calling to recap last night's highlights after the theater or dinner party.

I stood there for an hour. I stood there until all the faces blended together and the sweat made the back of my shirt stick to me like wet tissue paper. I think I would have stayed there all afternoon if I had known that she would eventually pass by. She was probably still at home. There was a comfort in knowing that her *home* meant that she was somewhere close to me. Even if I didn't know where that was exactly.

Astoria is littered with sidewalk cafes and there's always someone who feels that there's room for one more. I lost count of how many I passed while I walked aimlessly through the streets.

They were mostly Greek, but as I walked toward the elevated train on 28th Avenue I passed by Café Rover on 38th Street, the latest café endeavor. Glancing over the patrons occupying the tables, I saw a rather large group sitting at the end of the café, closest to the corner. Some of them were smoking cigarettes and the men were loudly laughing at each other, quoting random lines from *Goodfellas* and old Bugs Bunny cartoons. It was the blonde hair at the head of the table that stopped me cold. It was the back of one of the women's heads, but the hair color screamed at me that it was *her*. She wore a red shirt and her hair was styled the same way as the first time I saw her on the train. While I watched her, she flicked the ash off her cigarette and blew a white-gray cloud over their heads. My stomach went cold. I hadn't expected her to smoke, and I don't know why but I felt so disappointed.

She was leaning in to speak with one of the other women at the table while the men continued to discreetly ogle the waitress. The one she talked with smiled slightly and then took a drink out of something red in a glass. Somewhere inside, someone dropped a tray full of plates and everyone cheered. Everyone at her table lifted their glasses in a mock toast. I looked at the ground underneath her chair and saw that she was wearing thick-soled black boots. The man to her right turned to her and whispered something in her ear while he caressed her elbow.

"Can I help you, sir?" asked an eighteen-year-old girl in a tight, plaid schoolgirl skirt and a white top. I looked down at her blankly and asked her what she meant. "Uh…I was…just wondering if you would like a table?" A couple walked passed their table and stopped to say hello to them. She moved slightly and brushed some hair behind her left ear. They both bent down and gave her the obligatory hello kiss on the cheek. Ignoring the sweat on my forehead, I squinted and tried to bring her into focus. I still couldn't make out if it was her or not.

"Sir?" the girl asked. Looking over the hostess's head, I watched her stand up from the table and dust her lap. She turned profile suddenly and then looked in my direction, as she tried to find her waitress. It wasn't her. This girl was shorter by several inches and her nose was larger. She didn't even have the same build. No, it was just the hair. Of course it wasn't her, as if she would surround herself with a group like that. Getting together and drinking iced coffee, laughing so loud that people who walked across the street could hear you; it was unseemly. And smoking a cigarette! "No thanks," I told the hostess and kept walking toward the train.

I caught the bus home about half a mile down and my stop came up about ten minutes later. Hilda was sitting in a folding chair at the entrance to the apartment building, her black terrier dog, Cherry, sat next to her. "Hello Everest," she smiled.

"Hi Hilda." Hilda, as far I knew, was the oldest living tenant in my building. Actually, I think she was the oldest living tenant in Ravenswood. She lived on the third floor, and had been there for decades. Hilda's claim to fame was that she lived there when it was "a good neighborhood." Her husband died about five years prior and her children, grandchildren and great-grandchildren lived nearby. She knew everybody by name, including the gang-bangers that hung around the courtyard. A short, pudgy, black lady with a head full of short, thick white hair, Hilda only sat outside in the daytime and only spoke to people she knew.

"It's a beautiful day, isn't it?" she asked. Since she was a little hard of hearing, I waited to get next to her before I answered, Cherry's tail immediately began to wag and she came up to me. Occasionally, Hilda would ask me to walk Cherry when she wasn't feeling up to it and sometimes I dog sat for her whenever she visited family out of town. "Yeah it is. How've you been, Hilda?" I picked up Cherry and rubbed her head.

"Great, thanks. Any better and I'd start to worry. How about you?"

"Ok, thanks."

"You go shopping?"

"No, not really. Just decided to go out for a while."

"Day like today, I can't blame you."

"How are all the kids?"

"Oh fine, just fine, thank you." There was the inevitable silence that followed. I'm not a very good conversationalist, so I usually found myself stuck in awkward silences where nobody really knows what to say. At that point, I just wanted to go inside. Still, I didn't want to seem rude, so I hung around a bit longer. Plus, I liked Hilda and Cherry. "How's work?" she asked.

"Oh, it's...ok."

"Still dealing with those crazy customers?"

"Yeah."

"Can't be easy, a job like that. Still, you have to hang in there, you know. Lots of folks don't even have a job or the prospect of getting one."

"I know."

"It's rough all over, baby. Be grateful for what you got."

"I try. Hard sometimes," I answered, still petting Cherry.

"I know, I know. Say, would you mind walking Cherry later? My back's been acting up a little lately."

"Sure, no problem. Usual time, 7?"

"Yes, that's perfect. Thanks so much, baby."

I erased the message for Sanchez after leaving Hilda downstairs. She'd go inside as soon as the sun began to set. Out of my window, I saw that the people in the apartment directly across the courtyard from mine were getting ready to have another party. That would be one more night the cops would be down there. Simone walked out wearing a pair of cut off jeans and a black tee shirt. Hilda didn't bother to say hello. Soon, there were no more shadows in the courtyard. Sun went down. A group of kids in baggy clothes with du-rags on their heads walked onto the grounds from the other side of the buildings and Hilda folded up her chair and went inside. Neighbors were starting to argue and various, disembodied sounds bounced down the hallway. Soon there would be kids drinking by the curb as they listened to the Salsa and Rap music which boosted their enthusiasm. Angry, hopeful kids with cars, alcohol, and a lot of time to spare. Another summer night in Ravenswood. Be grateful for what you got, huh?

Chapter Eight

The N train pulled into Lexington at ten after six on Tuesday night. She walked on in mid-sentence, she wasn't alone. I looked up from the paper I was pretending to read and saw a fat brunette with a faint mustache and a tight black business getup follow her to two empty seats diagonally across from me. She was still wearing the Ray Bans, but that day she had on a conservative brown suit. They were facing the rear of the train, so I got up and rushed to take the empty seat directly behind her and almost knocked over a guy with a white turban that had hoped to sit down. I found myself wedged between the college student pouring over an economics textbook and the car's window. It was so goddamn noisy in the car I couldn't make out what she was saying or even what her voice was like. I felt like standing on my chair and screaming at all those assholes to shut the hell up. Instead, I closed my eyes and tilted my head back a little to try and get a whiff of her perfume.

The N jerked forward and then it slowly started to pull away from the station. "Thank you so much for recommending *Nicky's*. We had a great time," her fat, hairy friend said.

"Oh, did you like it?" Her voice. It was _her_ voice.

"Oh yes, it was fantastic. Thanks again."

"I'm glad. Did George like it?" She didn't have the slightest trace of an accent. Not the nasally, Fran Dreschner Queens pierce or the Rosy Perez Bronx drawl or the Long Island spoiled chirp. Not her.

"Oh, I guess. Honestly, he was really getting on my nerves."

"Really? I thought things were going well with him."

"They were and then all of a sudden, it happens."

"What happens?"

"The same thing that happens to most men after they have sex, Jekyll and Hyde syndrome. Except that Mr. Hyde is the one who's always around and Dr. Jekyll goes away," her friend said. She laughed at the comparison and my eyes closed as soon as I heard the sound. It was soft, but still rising above the steady percussion of the rails. "I'm sorry, Maggie."

"That's alright. I was waiting for it."

As the train emerged from the tunnel and came up in Queens, Maggie asked her a question just as the kid next to me sneezed on page 87 of _Understanding Economics, 4th Edition._ I didn't catch what she asked, but her answer was, "Good. Really good." That could've meant almost anything. What was good? I wondered. Lunch? A meeting at work with the boss? Her parents? Her...husband? While I waited for her to go into more detail, the girl sneezed again, this time covering her mouth. Nothing. They were quiet. Even when the train came to an abrupt stop and shook everybody on board, there was nothing. "Come on, Maggie, you fat fucking hairball, ask her for details!" I thought. The kid turned to me from her textbook. Had I said that *out loud*?

"Oh my God, did I tell you what happened today at lunch?" Maggie asked.

"Remember today I told you that I wanted to go to Bloomingdale's to pick up a tie for my father's birthday? Well, I went for lunch and - by the way did I tell you that they're having a great sale on shoes? I saw the cutest pair of pumps, but I just couldn't get them. I've already spent too much on clothes as it is. "Anyway, I was standing on line waiting and there was this guy, like, two people in front of me. From the sound of it, he was trying to return something but he was acting like a real ass."

"What do you mean?" she asked.

"He was giving the sales girl a really hard time. She was like, trying to calm him down and explain the return policy and he was just, like, going off on her and telling her that he didn't care what the damn policy was. Then he started cursing and yelling that he didn't have time for this shit, and that she was just a...what the hell did he say? Oh, that she was just a little sales clerk and that he made more money in a day than she probably did in a year, all this bullshit."

"Oh my God."

"Oh, you would've thought that she had spat at him or something, the way he was carrying on. Then he demanded to speak to her supervisor and started screaming for one right in front of everybody," Maggie went on.

"What a jerk!"

"The manager finally got there and this guy starts yelling at him too, saying the sales girl was useless and had been no help whatsoever. Meanwhile, she's standing there crying like a wimp."

"Maggie!"

"What? I'm just saying that if he had tried that kind of shit with me, they would've had to call security to pull me off him."

It's funny how brave people are when they're not the ones in the situation they're talking about. I noticed that while she was telling this whole story, she never once mentioned how she felt so bad for the sales girl that she intervened on her behalf and put that asshole in his place. If she had been so appalled by his behavior, why did she let it go on? I guess for some people it's just easier to talk about how they would react *if* something happened to them than it is to actually do something when they see it happen to someone else. They won't tolerate it, but it's perfectly acceptable to stand there and watch it happen to someone else.

"God, why do people have to act like that? Especially over something so trivial like that! I mean, is it really worth making her cry?! That man's life isn't on the line or anything if Bloomingdale's has to give him a store credit for a return. There are worse things than getting stuck with credit for Bloomingdales. Poor thing, I feel so bad for her," she said. Maggie just sat there and didn't say anything. Of course she didn't say anything. I don't really think that Maggie had the capacity to understand what she was talking about. Kindness, understanding, compassion. Things Maggie probably never thought about. But she did.

She was going to get off at Astoria Boulevard which was the following stop. I didn't want to let her go yet. The train started slowing down. She and Maggie were getting their things together to get off. Next thing I knew, I got up and stood by the door. When I glanced over to my left, there was a guy sitting there staring at their feet. He wasn't even trying to be discreet about it, his mouth was opened. She and Maggie seemed not to notice, though. Maggie had gone off about something else and I noticed the small beads of sweat glistening on the hairs above her lip. How could she be friends with someone like Maggie? She probably felt bad for Maggie and so she let her tag along sometimes. I noticed the guy had shifted himself in his seat while staring at Maggie's black flats standing next to her black pumps. All I wanted to do was bash his head against the wall.

They walked out of the car and right before I followed, I looked down at the fetish pervert and shook my head as his eyes remained glued to their shoes, the silent debasement obvious in a smirk at the corner of his mouth. "Sick," I said, just before the doors closed

behind me. Not wanting to see that stupid, surprised look on his

goddamn face, I stepped up to catch up to her, but still kept a

respectable distance. I didn't want to get too close. Who knows

what she would think if she saw me behind her.

When we got to the Boulevard, she said goodbye to Maggie and

started to walk toward Astoria Park. Next to us, rush hour traffic

was filled with frustrated commuters hoping to move five inches

closer to getting on the Triborough Bridge, literally a few feet away.

There was a small kids' playground on our right called Hoyt Park

that was filled with children and teenagers laughing and playing on

the swings or chasing each other up and down a small basketball

court. On the corner, across the street, there were two three-story

apartment buildings next to a larger apartment complex that

stretched all the way down the block to the other avenue. She

walked across the street and stopped in front of the first three-story

building. It was white with black painted windows and ledges and a

glass door leading into the small lobby. There was an old man with a walker out front talking to an old lady who watched her grandson play with a small airplane.

She hadn't seen me, so I stood by this parked car at the corner of the park. Once she went inside, I saw her check her mailbox before she disappeared up the stairs. Walking away from the mini-van I was hiding behind, I started toward the building and waited until the old couple walked away. All the windows on the second floor had the shades drawn so I figured if she lived there, I wouldn't be able to see her. I moved down the alley and toward the back of the building where I saw a fire escape. For a second, I considered climbing it, but then I realized that it was still broad daylight and someone could see me.

She said she felt sorry for the girl at Bloomingdale's. More than likely, that asshole who yelled at her would probably wind up calling their corporate office to complain about the service he got. This girl did her job and followed their policy and this jerk-off who was oh-so-inconvenienced by it all is actually going to take time out of his day to call and register a complaint. It's not enough that he had her in tears and held everybody up on line, oh no. No, he's going to drive the point home and show what a big, tough man he is and register his complaint. I could see it happening. And the sad part is that people like him, whom I've come to believe now encompass most of the world, will never see just how petty and ridiculous their complaints really are.

But not her. She seemed to actually understand and would never do something like that. I wondered how many times she'd been inconvenienced at some commercial level and she probably never bothered to call. I doubted that the phrase, "I'll never shop in your store again and I'm gonna tell everybody I know to do the same" had ever escaped those soft lips. And not because she was a pushover, as some of these "people," for lack of a better word, would say. But because she knew that in the grand scheme of things, it really wasn't that important. It wasn't brain surgery, nobody was going to die if they couldn't return a sweater or a book or whatever. It wasn't a crime against God and man if every single spoiled want, need, or desire wasn't met at every single instant of their lives. Jesus, the simple gesture of giving Ben her sandwich said that she understood that. Her earlier statement to Maggie nailed it down. How could I not follow her? How could I not want to talk to someone like that?

A light came on somewhere on the third floor. When I walked back down the alley, I saw that it was somebody's kitchen. Seconds later, she was at the window, flipping through mail before looking like she threw it away in the garbage. She turned off the light and went to another room, but I couldn't tell where. I ran toward the back again, the light came on at the window, but I still couldn't see her. Going from the side to the back didn't seem to help and there were no other angles where I could get a look, other than climbing the fire escape. Of course, I would have to jump and grab the bottom rung to pull myself up, but I knew I could make it. I wasn't that badly out of shape. While I stood there thinking about it, though, I noticed a face peeked at me from behind the shade on the second floor. When they noticed that I had seen them, they turned from the window and I ran for the Boulevard.

Chapter Nine

By blind, stupid luck, I got to the station in time to hop on an N right before the doors closed. There was only one more stop, so there weren't that many people in the car. I was sweating and panting like I was about to pass out. God, I couldn't believe it! Somebody had actually seen me. I started to wonder what would happen if they told her that they saw someone staring up at her apartment?! What if they described who they saw and she realized that it was me?! I didn't think that they had gotten that good a look at me. Then again, I had no idea how long they had watched me. Whoever it was had to be a neighbor of hers' and they could feel the need to tell her what they saw, just for her own safety. *"This is going to ruin everything!"*

I paced around my apartment for half an hour when I got home. I was so nervous that I couldn't even eat. Everything was fine until I pulled that stupid follow-her-home stunt. Even then though, I couldn't help but think how beautiful she looked. I would've loved to have seen her at home, relaxed and laid back. As I walked from room to room, I began to wonder what she did when she was at home. How would someone like her pass the time?

I avoided taking the train at the same time in the days that followed. Either I left at the exact time that I was supposed to, which really seemed to irk George, or if it turned out that I had to stay late, I'd hang out at the bookstore for a while. At least an hour or so, until I was sure that she had already taken the ride home. Even then, I got on at the other end of the train. Who knew how she would react if it turned out that her nosy fucking neighbor saw me and told her that I was there? Maybe she'd call the police. I figured that the best thing to do would be to lie low, although the thought of not seeing her depressed me.

The phone rang and I wind up having to talk to a college professor who is vehemently opposed to the way we "lump the classics of literature together with the dribble that's churned out these days." When I asked what he was referring to specifically, he sighed and told me that if he had to explain it to me then I was obviously not the person that he needed to speak with. "What's your CEO's name?"

"Peter Callahan, sir, but – "

"And what's the address where I am may write him?" I gave him the address and tried to explain that any letters that are sent to Mr. Callahan are addressed by the customer service department and that since I had him on the phone, I would be glad to help him. "No, you're not high up enough on the ladder to make any kind of effective change in things. I'll write to Mr. Callahan."

When I hung up, George was standing right behind me. "Can I see you for a second, Everest?" George closed his door when we walked in and took a minute to check his e-mail before turning to me again. "I wanted to talk to you about something that's concerning me."

"What is it?"

"Well, Everest, let me first ask you if everything's ok? Is there…anything wrong or anything you'd like to talk about?"

"Um…no, George. I…I don't think so. Why?"

"The reason I'm asking is because I've noticed a slight…decline in your performance lately."

"Really?"

"Yes. You don't…seem like yourself, lately. You seem to be distracted, irritable."

"Irritable?"

"It's been noticed by people around the office."

"Really? I…don't know what to say. What's been said?"

"That you don't seem like yourself."

"Well, is there a specific instance that they're referring to? I mean, I barely even talk to-"

"It's just lately, that's all, Everest. Even I've heard you get a little…testy with the customers. Sometimes, people have heard you…talking to yourself."

I tried to think of the last few conversations with customers that I had had but nothing came to mind. He said that people around the office had noticed a change in my attitude, but how could that be when I barely spoke to anyone except Floyd, really. And I doubted that he would have said something like that. In terms of talking to myself, maybe I had been so preoccupied with almost getting caught, that I hadn't realized what I was saying out loud. I made a mental note that I had to watch out for that. "I'm…sorry, George. I certainly don't mean to get testy. Could you give me an example?"

"Just in the way your tone of voice changes when you're on the phone with someone who it seems you're not getting through to. I've noticed it myself when I've passed by"

"Ah, I don't know what to say. I hadn't realized."

"That's why I'm bringing it up. I thought maybe we'd talk about it." He was giving me the concerned manager act. It came out every once in a while, usually when someone's had a death in the family.

We sat in silence for a while. The phones weren't too bad and he just kept staring at me, waiting for me to say something. I think he was waiting for me to admit that I was using drugs or was having some kind of family problem or something. How could I tell him what was really bothering me? I hadn't seen her in a few days and I had to alter my whole daily routine because somebody in her building may have reported me lurking around the alley. I stared at his desk for a while and hoped that someone would call him. "Are you getting tired of the job?" he asked.

Yes. "No," I answered, trying not to hesitate. Of course I was tired of the job. I was tired of the ridiculous, pathetic complaints I dealt with, I was tired of looking at that stupid cubicle wall, tired of apologizing. But what was I going to do? Look for another job? That was easier said than done. I tried looking through the want ads and it just made me dizzy. Most of the jobs I did qualify for were basically photocopies of what I was doing already. My history was in serving the consumer in one way or another. Every other place wanted some type of background or experience in a specific field. I had even filled out applications with a few employment agencies, interviewed with a couple of them, but none ever got back to me. Since I didn't seem to be getting anywhere with anyone, and I obviously couldn't afford to lose my job, what else could I tell George but, "No, not at all. I really…like my job."

He sat back in his "captain's chair" and checked his e-mail again. "Listen, you're up for review in two months. I'd hate to see you going down this path. Do you think you can get it together before then?" I nodded. "Good. Look, I know that this job can get monotonous sometimes, but you gotta keep giving the same, consistent service to everybody that calls, you know?"

"Yes. Sorry, George. I'll try."

"And remember, people notice things around here. If you look unhappy, people around here will notice it and they'll start talking and it just doesn't look good. For you or for the department."

"Right."

"Tell you what. How about if I start giving you some more e-mails to do and that way, you're not on the phones as much? Naturally, you'll still have to back up Sofia and Brian, but at least it'll be a switch from the ordinary. Does that make sense?"

After I thanked him for trying to help me, I went back to my desk and readied myself for the next phone call. George said that he would start shooting some e-mails over to me that afternoon, so I put on my headset to back up Brian and Sofia.

About a half hour later, George came out of his office and told us that he had a meeting to go to and that if we needed him, he'd be in the conference room. As soon as he left, Sofia took off her headset and went to the break room for some coffee. "Everything ok?" asked Brian. He and Sofia were probably wondering what George had called me in the office for.

"Yeah, thanks."

"George mentioned that he was going to start giving you some more e-mails from now on."

"Yeah, that's what we were talking about in his office."

"What we really need around here is another rep."

"Mmm."

"I mean, it's just us for the entire country," he looked around to see if anyone else was around, "and George doesn't even really speak to the customers or answer e-mails," he whispered. Sofia showed up just then, carrying a cup of coffee and a bag of cheese doodles. She offered me some, but I shook my head. Brian grabbed a few.

"How's it going, guys?" she asked.

"Just commenting how we could really use another body around here."

"Oh God, yes," she said. "Is that what you and George were talking about, Everest?"

"No, that was nothing. We were just going over some things. No biggie."

"George is going to start giving Everest more e-mails," Brian said.

"Really? That's interesting," her eyes wandered away, sort of glazed. She couldn't have been more obvious if she had "BORED SHITLESS" stamped on her forehead. The phone rang just then and Brian went to answer it.

At five o'clock, it was time to shut down the computer, turn off the monitor, ignore George's disapproving sigh and leave. Brian left at about a quarter after four and I was stuck covering for him on the phone after he left. Before that, George came through on his promise and had been giving me e-mails to respond to for the bulk of the day.

Steve Giropolous spotted me from the back of the train car and smiled as he walked up to me. I hadn't seen Steve since I started working at Astor House. He and I went to high school together. We got along ok. He used to be on the wrestling team at Long Island City High. I was on the debate team. Odd pairing, but we would hang out occasionally. "I can't believe this! Everest Porter. Man, how are you?"

"Ok, thanks. How are you, Steve?" I was actually glad to see him. It broke the monotony of staring at everyone's dumb face for the day, especially since I wasn't able to see her. Steve hadn't changed. He still looked like he was wrestling, even in the double-breasted suit. "Good, thanks."

"Where are you working now? Are you still over at that advertising company?"

"Wayne, Schwartz and Geller. Yeah, it's my ninth year now with them."

"Wow."

"Yeah, it's a good company to work for. How about you? Last time I bumped into you, you were a waiter at uh…oh what was the name of that place?"

"Cyprus."

"Right. Still there?"

"No, actually I had just left the last time I saw you to work for Astor House Books."

"Oh! That's right. Sorry, I've got a really bad memory."

"That's ok." I noticed the wedding band on his finger. It was a quiet, simple gold band. "Congratulations are in order I see," motioning toward his finger.

"Hmm? Oh, thanks. Yeah, I tied the knot about two years ago."

"That's great."

"Yeah, she's fantastic. What about you? Married?"

"No. Just me."

"Oh. Well – " Why do people's voices usually trail off after you say "no" to that question?

"Hey, you know I thought I saw you the other day. I was walking home and I thought I saw you running down Astoria Boulevard." Suddenly, I found myself staring at him. He had seen me running? Was it possible he had seen me run out of the alley? "Really?" I asked.

"Yeah, but I wasn't sure if it was you or not."

"I…doubt it. I get off at Ditmars."

"Oh, then it couldn't have been you."

"You still around the neighborhood then?"

"Yeah, not too far from the folks, you know. I had accepted this position with the company out of their Boston office a few years ago and met my wife there. When another position became available here, I wanted to come back home and she followed, of course. We just moved back a couple of weeks ago. We have a house over on 26th between Astoria Boulevard and 24th Avenue."

I started to feel really uncomfortable and I remember hoping that it wouldn't show. "So what are you doing at Astor House?"

"I work in customer service."

"Oh, so you're the guy that gets to talk to all the customers, right?"

"Yeah."

"Well, that can't be too fun. I can only imagine the kind of calls you get."

"It's not easy sometimes."

"I mean, I think I have it bad when I have to talk to more than five people all day, including clients. How many calls do you get a day?"

"Uh, I don't know really. I don't keep track. A lot." I had started to sweat.

"You see any of the guys from school?"

"No. You?"

"Not since the reunion."

"Reunion?"

"Yeah, we had a ten year reunion three years ago. Didn't you get the invitation?"

"No."

"Oh. Well…" There was the trail again. "It was no big deal, really. A bunch of people from L.I.C. met up at the gymnasium. The food was horrible. I think they had the same stuff they slopped out in the cafeteria." I smiled but it was more because we had pulled into Astoria Boulevard rather than his joke.

"Hey listen, let me give you my card. We should keep in touch." So he gave me his fucking card and for a second, I thought I saw her standing behind him. I kind of jumped a little, startling Steve. "What's the matter, it's not that impressive of a title," he joked. His card read that he was a Regional Manager for the Northeast district. When I looked over his shoulder again, there wasn't anyone there and that's when I started to worry. "Uh…no, it's not that. I uh…forget it. Thanks for the card."

"Sure. You ok?"

"Yeah, I'm fine, thanks. So listen, I'll give you a call sometime."

"Great. You'll come over for dinner and meet the wife. Here, let me write down our home number."

"Sounds good."

Chapter Ten

I couldn't focus on anything the next day at work. If somebody who I hadn't seen in years thought they recognized me the other day while I was running, I was sure that someone else could have been able to make out my face. Maybe they even reported me to the cops. I pictured it going down like something out of a bad movie. There I would be, sitting in my cube, talking to some son of a bitch out in Westbumblefuck USA and the next thing I know, some cop would be right behind me, at the ready to slap the cuffs on and haul me down to the station or wherever the fuck they take you. And George, Captain Marvel, arms folded across his chest while he smirked right behind him, just happier than a pig in shit about how they finally took me off his hands.

Even though I had desperately tried to make sure I wouldn't bump into her, when I got out of work on a Friday night and the train was getting close to 59th and Lexington, I had moved to the front of the car, the same car as the other times. I wanted to see her, or rather…I needed to see her. Either way, she was all I thought about and it had been too long since I had seen her last. Besides, I started to doubt that anyone had taken notice of me that time in the alley.

Certainly, nobody had gotten enough of a description of me to track

me down. I had to see her. It had felt like months since the last

time. What if she had changed her schedule? What if she got some

big promotion at work and she had to change her hours so that now,

she wouldn't take the same train? What if she just had other plans?

Everybody crowded in and people grimaced at each other as they

squeezed past. At the other end of the car, I saw the blonde hair. It

was her. It was *her*. When she looked up, I saw the Ray Bans and I

realized that it was really her. I couldn't remember the last time I

felt so happy. Actually, happy isn't really the word. No, I

was...relieved. As if a big weight had been taken off me and I was

able to take a deep breath for the first time in ages. Everything else

around me drowned out and I felt my shoulders drop, even though

the train was more full than usual. She kind of smiled at someone as

she edged past them and tried to make her way through the crowd so

she could hold onto the bar. That smile, so pure it was like a child's

dream.

Little by little, people emptied out of the car. Nobody new came on and before I knew it, we were sitting across from each other. I moved a little closer at every stop. She still hadn't noticed me. Why would she? Who the hell was I?

The train stopped midway to Astoria Boulevard. I tried really hard not to stare, but I couldn't help it. She wore a smooth tailored red suit that matched the color of her nails and a white top, pearls under the collar. With the exception of a guy who slept in a seat in the corner, we were the only ones in the car. All I wanted was to say something to her, perhaps start a conversation that could lead to something more. And that was the perfect situation for something like that to happen. We were stuck, we were pretty much alone, why not? I tried to think of something clever to say when I realized that she'd probably heard everything a million times before. How many more interesting ways are there to say "Hi"? Suddenly, her face turned slightly toward me.

The train began to crawl toward Astoria Boulevard and we finally got to the station. She gathered herself together and smiled at me as she got up to leave. When the doors opened, she walked out not noticing that she had dropped a piece of yellow paper on the floor. That was it! That was my chance, my "in." I picked it up and just as I was getting out, the doors slid closed and I got stuck in between them. "Ms! Ms!" I called out. She turned around and I tried to act as cool as I could while being trapped halfway between the car and the platform, struggling with the doors. You'd think that after a minute or two, the conductor or whoever would open them again, right? Wrong. Instead, the doors just opened and closed again really fast so whatever's jammed them gets pounded pretty well, which was exactly what happened to me.

"I'm...sorry to bother...you, Ms., but you...dropped something." She looked down the platform and slowly took a step towards me. "What?" she asked.

"You uh...dropped something. I'd give it to...you, but ah...as you can...see, the hand that...has it, is still inside...the car." As she came closer, the doors suddenly opened and I stumbled out, landing on the floor in front of her. "Are you okay?" she knelt down and helped me on my feet. I looked over at her legs. "Yeah...I'm okay. It's nothing really. Thanks."

"I'm sorry, did you say that I dropped something?"

"Oh, yeah. Here." I gave her the paper and she unfolded it. "I know how frustrating it can be when you loose something."

"This is my dry cleaning ticket. Thank you so much."

"Oh, that's ok. Really, I'm just glad that I could…uh, you know, I'm glad I could help."

"I'm afraid that you missed your train." I hadn't even noticed that the train had left the station.

"That's okay. There'll be another one."

"I feel so bad, though. You got mangled by the doors, you fell and then you missed your train just for a dry cleaning ticket," she said sweetly.

"Well, I thought that, uh, I thought that it was important, you know? And it turns out that it is, because you wouldn't have been able to get your clothes back without that, right?"

"Right, but…I still feel bad."

"Please, don't. It's okay, really."

She was even more amazing up close than I had ever imagined. I kept wishing that she would take off her sunglasses. That would've been perfect. The voice, the fair skin, and the perfume…it was intoxicating. "What's your name?" she asked.

"Uh, Everest. Everest Porter."

"I'm Elsa Graham. It's nice to meet you." When I shook her hand, whatever idea I had of her skin being smooth was tossed out the window. Smooth couldn't describe it. Her hand was cool and softer than anything I had ever touched. It was so much more exciting than satin, but not as run-in-the-mill as silk. It was like dipping your hand into a bucket of cold water on a day when it's 95 degrees in the shade. You felt it all over your body.

"Well, Everest, thanks again for going through all this trouble. I really appreciate it. Hey, who says chivalry is dead, huh?" I think I nodded and managed to give her a weak smile. I let go as soon as I realized that I was still shaking her hand. "I have to get going. Sorry again about your train."

"Oh, it's nothing, really. Glad I could be of service."

"Take care."

"I…I guess I'll…see you on the train…sometime." She smiled and turned toward the staircase.

I must've looked like an idiot on the bus ride home, smiling at everyone. Nobody sat next to me. God, she was incredible. She was everything that I thought she would be and more. And I even knew her name! We, both of us, knew each other's names! Elsa. Elsa Graham. Elsa. Now, the next time I would see her, I could actually go over and say hello. We could have a conversation! I could walk over and sit next to her, watch those other assholes salivate and envy me while we talked about each other's day and maybe even talk about getting together for a drink on the way home. Now that's what I would call "happy hour."

Hilda was sitting outside the building again. "Well hello, Everest! You sure look different today."

"I do?"

"Yes, you sure do. You're smiling. I don't think I've ever seen you do that before." She was right, I was still smiling.

"Aw, come on."

"No, I'm serious. What happened, get some good news at work today?"

"Pssh! Now that would be something if work could make me smile." I knelt down and played with Cherry.

"Oh, it must be a woman, then huh? Yeah, that's one of the only things that'll make a man smile like that. I mean, unless you're gay or somethin'."

"You're pretty sharp, Hilda."

"Aint got nothin' to do with that. It's experience. When my son first met his wife, he came home with a smile from ear to ear. I never saw him smile like that before. Just the way you're smilin' now."

"Well to be honest, yeah. It's a woman. The most amazing woman I've ever met in my life."

"Ooo, listen to that! You got it bad, don't you? Ha!"

"I guess, yeah," my face was starting to hurt from smiling but I didn't care. "Her name is Elsa and she's sweet and caring and has a big heart."

"That's great, baby."

"She's really smart too and…well she's the most beautiful woman I've seen."

"Oh you're done, aren't you? You're all in, Everest," she smiled.

"Yeah," I sighed. "I think I am."

"Well she sounds like a great lady."

"She definitely is, yeah."

"Good, I'm happy for you. It's not every day you meet someone like that."

"No, it isn't. Need me to walk Cherry later?"

"Well, if you wouldn't mind."

"No, of course not. I'll be by at 7."

My head was racing. I kept on going over the whole scene again and again. Everything from when she smiled at me to just before she got off. I started to think that maybe when she dropped her dry cleaning ticket, it hadn't been by accident. Maybe she wanted me to get it back to her. I mean, it was pretty coincidental that she happened to drop her ticket in front of me on her way out. And, she obviously had noticed that I was looking at her because she smiled at me before she left. Maybe that was her way of getting me to talk to her. Maybe she knew somehow that I wanted to, but I just couldn't think of anything to say because she was so beautiful and this was her way of letting me know that it was ok; that I didn't have to be shy. The whole thing seemed too fantastic to be true. And she even asked for my name!

I couldn't keep still. I kept going around in circles in the apartment. It suddenly seemed so small. It was like the walls were closing in on me. It was getting hard to breathe. I began to wonder what she was doing. I wondered if she was home, which wasn't too far from my place. Was she thinking about what happened? Did she remember what I looked like? Was she wondering what I was doing? It was driving me nuts. I turned on the T.V., but I couldn't concentrate on what was on. I tried to watch a couple of boring reruns, the news; it was like everyone spoke gibberish. Nothing was sinking in. I turned it off after a while and opened the window.

The air felt good. It was muggy though, with a slight stench from all the crap that got churned out from the factories nearby. Still, it felt good against my face. The more I thought about her, the more I leaned out of the window. I wanted to yell at the top of my lungs. I would probably have gotten shot. When I leaned out more, I was practically halfway out, I closed my eyes and drew in a deep, long breath. Although it felt like my lungs would explode, I still couldn't get enough air in. I wanted more. Just a few floors below me, the street was waking up. I didn't want to look at any of it. Instead, I turned around and looked straight up, past the windows, over the roof, right into a coal-gray sky. The paper that morning said it would rain. I could almost taste it in the air, it was a wet tease of what was coming. My arms stretched out, I leaned out a little more and felt my feet just barely lift off the floor. For a second, with my eyes closed and the air hitting me just so, it felt like I was flying. God, it was great. Even the sounds of the neighborhood were different in that moment. With the whole world turned upside-down, I thought about Elsa and how she was the one who brought this out in me. When I slowly opened my eyes, I couldn't help but let out a small laugh.

A loud knock on my door almost made me loose my balance and fall out the window. I waved my arms in circles and jerked myself forward until I was back inside, down on all fours. It wouldn't have taken much for me to go in the other direction. Now that would've been embarrassing. The knock came again so I stood up and got myself together. "Who is it?"

"It's Hilda. You didn't come by to pick up Cherry so I wanted to make sure everything was okay." I looked at the time and realized that it was 7:30! I hadn't realized that so much time had gone by.

"I'm so sorry, Hilda. I lost track of time," I said, opening the door.

"It's okay, I just got worried since you're always on time," she waited by the door with Cherry on her leash while I got my keys.

"I was just...never mind," I smiled and walked to the elevator with Hilda.

"Boy, I guess this really must be some woman that's got your mind so busy," she laughed. I nodded, laughing as well.

Usually, I walked Cherry around the block until she did her business and then it was back to the building. That night, though, I felt so excited that I walked her all the way to Astoria Boulevard. When I stopped at the corner, I looked in the direction of her building and thought about walking over. I imagined bumping into her and watching her gush over Cherry. We would talk about the neighborhood and I would ask her out to dinner. I really felt like the possibilities were endless.

After I dropped off Cherry, I apologized to Hilda again and then went to my apartment. Back on the couch, I couldn't concentrate on anything. Each time I changed the channel, I remembered something about her. Channel 7 had some bullshit Disney Friday night teen show and I thought about the way she smiled at me before she got off the train. On Channel 4, I remembered the way she said her name. Channel 11, I thought about the suit she wore. I remembered how her red high heels clicked on the subway floor and I started to imagine how she might have gotten dressed that day. She probably picked everything out the night before so that in the morning, she wouldn't have to rush. What would the morning be like for her? I thought of a large bedroom with a king sized canopy bed against the wall. After a shower, I imagined her wearing a pair of white satin panties, not a thong, but panties and I got hard right away. I pictured her slowly sliding on those white stockings with a lace pattern at the top and I barely noticed when I undid my pants. Then maybe she'd put on a white lace bra and take a minute to look at herself in a full-body mirror in the corner of her room. How could she avoid that? My breathing got heavier as my hand moved faster and right just then I could see her perfectly. She was staring at herself, moving her hands over her body, adjusting the stockings, hooking the bra in the back, admiring the lift it gave her perfectly shaped breasts. I started to sweat. Maybe she finished doing her hair, applying what little make up she wore. Just before she got her suit out of the closet, perhaps she turned around and pulled the panties down slightly over each cheek. As she spread the cool satin over her skin, she couldn't avoid smiling as she looked at the perfectly round symmetry of her ass. My heart felt like it was going to burst out of my chest and I actually thought that I was going to hyperventilate. The pants came on first then, one slender leg at a time. Then the blouse, buttons, the heels and the jacket. As she took one last look at herself, I felt my body tense up and start to shake. When she put on the Ray Bans and smiled, my eyes rolled back into my head as the rest of me went into spasms.

Chapter Eleven

Once my head cleared, I cleaned myself up and jumped in the shower. While I scrubbed myself and lathered up, I started to think about what I had just done. I took the only pure thing in my life and turned it into something completely perverted. Here was this beautiful, incredible woman and I turned her into a wet dream. God, I started to feel like I was no better than all those other assholes on the train that probably went home and fantasized about her the same way, or in some cases maybe even worse! Who knows what kind of sick situations she had lived out for these scumbags in their minds? Here I went and fell right in line with them.

When I got dressed and walked into the kitchen, I was about to throw away the Q-Tips I finished using and when I opened the garbage, I saw the tissues I had used to clean myself up after I was done on the couch. They were lying there on top of what was left of that morning's breakfast. A loud reminder of the "tribute" I had paid her. What would she think of me if she knew what I'd done? I mean Jesus, other men write poetry or paint a portrait or write a song about the woman they can't get out of their head and what did I do? I jerked off in my living room.

The weekend was boring as usual. Got up on Saturday, did the laundry, listened to the neighbors drown out my T.V., fell asleep on the couch. Repeat on Sunday, replacing laundry with grocery shopping for an added twist. Sometimes, I was almost grateful when Monday came along. That is, until I got about a block away from the office and I realized that I was just changing the scenery. Same ol' shit, different cubicle.

The first few calls that came in were nothing. People calling to say that they would like to see a store open in their community, someone else called to let us know about the great service they got, somebody else wanted to let us know that they really liked the coffee in the cafes and that the bathrooms were always so "clean and shiny".

When there were a few minutes where the phones didn't ring, Brian finally turned around and told me that he was leaving.

"What?"

"I quit. I just told George this morning."

"Really?"

"I got a better offer somewhere else."

"That's great," I said. Sofia walked in just then and came right over when she saw us talking. "What's up?" she asked.

"I was just telling Everest that I gave George my two weeks notice this morning."

"Wow. Really?"

"Yeah."

"Well...um, wow. Are...are you going somewhere else?" she asked.

"I got an offer to be the manager of this new boutique that's opening up in Midtown."

"So you're staying in retail," she said.

"Yeah. But, at least I won't have to listen to these psychos anymore," he motioned toward the phone. "It'll be different."

George came over and Sofia made room for him to pass by. He stopped at his door and asked Brian if he had given us "the news."

"Yeah, I just told them."

"Well, it'll be hard to replace you, Brian but…we'll try," he smiled, trying to sound lighthearted. "Seriously though, I'm sorry to see you go."

Later on while Brian was at lunch, Sofia came over to my cube. "So what do you think?"

"Huh?"

"You know, about Brian leaving. Something, huh?"

"Yeah."

"I'm so happy for him."

"Me too."

"I never saw it coming, though. I thought he would stay and try to go for another department."

"Well, nobody's taking on anyone new here."

"That's true. He was starting to get tired of this, though."

"You think so?"

"Yeah, I could tell. He would just be slumped over his desk the whole day, barely getting anything done. It was time for him to move on."

"I uh…I guess so."

"I think we should do something for him, you know? Like a cake or something."

George came over and asked what we were doing. Sofia stiffened up and told him that she was asking my opinion about whether or not we should buy a cake for Brian on his last day. "Oh. Well…I don't see why not. On his last day, you go out and pick up a cake and we'll all chip in for it." She nodded and went back to her cube.

Brian spent the whole day smiling. He answered most of the calls that came in with a real perky attitude and why not? What did he care? He would be gone in two weeks and wouldn't have to deal with those animals anymore. He stopped putting his head in his hands and just had a smirk the whole time. I admit that I was pretty jealous. It must feel really good to know that you're leaving a place like that. Kind of like knowing you're getting paroled, I would imagine.

The phone rang at 4:58 and I looked over at Brian, but he was already on the phone. Reluctantly, I picked it up and it was a customer in Illinois who insisted he was being discriminated against as a black man because even though he didn't have a receipt, the store was refusing to give him a cash refund on some books he wanted to return. After telling him that it was our policy not to provide cash refunds without a receipt, he became belligerent, demanded that I give him the name of my supervisor and kept me on for a few minutes to let me know what a racist company I worked for and that this wouldn't be the last of this. It was a quarter after five by the time he hung up on me. I walked into George's office and told him what happened. He agreed that it was probably a con and that he would probably call back, not realizing that we're actually a very small department and that Sofia was the only person left to answer the phones. We both told her about what happened and sure enough, just as I was almost done telling her, the phone rang again and the caller ID showed that it was from the same Illinois area code that had come up when I took the call. Sofia nodded after she answered to let us know that it was him.

Since he was now Sofia and George's problem, I shut everything down and took off. On the train ride home, I thought that I had probably missed my chance at catching Elsa. When I didn't see her get on at 59th Street, I realized that I was right. If I could just be around her, it would be enough to make me forget about all the shit from work. She offered the chance to see that there was at least one person out there that was different. There was somebody out there who wasn't looking to get away with something, who wasn't petty, somebody who actually cared about people. Thanks to that idiot who called and took up so much of my time, I missed the chance to see her. I got so angry that I felt my teeth grind together. We came up on Astoria Boulevard and I got out and made my way down to the street.

When I got the park across the street from her building, I tried to blend in and make it seem like I was really interested in the basketball game that was going on. A few minutes later, I saw her come out of her building, talking to some guy. I tried not to stare, but there they were, standing right by the door. He was a little shorter than her and had a beer belly that made it seem more like he was pregnant than anything else. She touched his arm at one point when they shared a laughed and I swear I felt my face get hot. He was balding, had a bad comb-over and a thick black moustache that practically covered his whole mouth. There was no way that he could be involved with someone like her. He looked greasy, even from where I stood. A few minutes later, a woman, slightly older than Elsa, came out and greeted her. They shook hands and then the woman and the fat guy with the moustache walked away while Elsa walked up the block.

Neighbors. Of course, they were neighbors. And it would make sense that she talked with them. I felt so stupid. I didn't even know what was going on, and already I was putting him in bed with her. Slowly, I walked away from the basketball court and out of the park, making my way up the block, but staying on the other side of street. Every once in a while, I looked over my shoulder to make sure that there was nobody watching me watching her. When she stopped to say hello to some other people that she met halfway up, I pretended to tie my laces.

It wasn't hard to spot her, even when she crossed the street ahead of me. She was so tall and that blonde hair stood out against everything else around her. I noticed that as she walked, she took long, graceful strides. There was a grocery store around the corner that she went into and I followed her, keeping a safe distance. While I waited outside, I looked down the block and over my shoulders, hoping that Steve or anyone else for that matter didn't see me out there waiting.

She came out a few minutes later carrying a paper bag. I pretended to read the menu of a Chinese take-out place on the corner and when she passed by, I waited until she was a good few cars down from the light before crossing the street and headed toward the park again. Some kids ran past her and she smiled at them. She didn't see me, but I was able to catch it. There was nothing I wouldn't give to see her smile at me again. I think I would trade everything I had if I could just sit down with her, have some coffee and talk about things. Nothing specifically, just things that make up a normal conversation with someone who isn't complaining about some nonsense or spreading some office gossip. Just two people talking about the things that normal, good people talk about. I was sure that she did that all the time. You could see it in the way she talked with her neighbors, or the way she smiled at those kids. Yeah, I would have given anything to have that. Even for just a second.

When I got to the middle of the block, I stopped walking. I didn't want to run the risk of someone spotting me so I just watched her until she disappeared inside her building. Even after I couldn't see her anymore, I still leaned against a parked car and stared at the front door. Just the idea of her was enough at the moment. Just remembering her that last split second before she went inside, that was good. I closed my eyes and tried to run the entire scene again through my mind. Watching her walk out, walking up the block and down again. Then I thought that maybe I should've offered to help her with her bag. Maybe she would've been so grateful that she would've invited me inside for a cold drink. I realized how stupid that sounded and shook the notion out of my head.

I fed off of that memory all the way home and past midnight. Every step, every movement was…perfection. Prior to that night, I hadn't considered getting a cell phone because, quite frankly, I didn't have anyone to call. But they had so many other functions that I started to look them up online and decided that I would pick up an iPhone the next day. I could see her in my mind, but with a picture…with a picture it was like I could have part of her with me, a small piece of her stolen from time near me.   Whenever things got too crazy, I could just pull out her picture and remember that she was out there. Elsa was out there and things then wouldn't seem that bad. Was that too creepy?

The following day I bought an iPhone and started going through all the features. It's not so easy to take a picture of someone without them knowing that they're being photographed, unless you're good at surveillance or something. I tested it out with a few random shots on the way home and then printed them out on my computer. Skinny blonde woman picking up her French poodle's sidewalk bomb, homeless guy slumped against the outside of a McDonald's, a family crossing the street together. Each shot came out crystal clear. I was just hoping that the ones I wanted to take of her would come out as clear.

My chance to find out finally came one day when I was going home and I saw her get on. She sat down at the other end of the car and took out *Tuesdays with Morrie* by Mitch Albom. I recognized the cover. God, she looked great. I hadn't seen her wearing that outfit before. It was a beautiful, dark gray, pinned-striped suit. There were too many people around though, so I felt that I couldn't just take out the phone and start snapping away. I figured I'd wait until Astoria Boulevard and then take a picture. As I thought about it, I felt my hands start to shake a little.

"Astoria Boulevard, change here for the N or the W going to Manhattan." The doors opened, I stood halfway out the doors and pointed the camera down the platform. Elsa walked out and I waited. I wanted just the right shot. There were some people who walked behind her and were in the way. As she walked toward the stairs, I was able to get a clear shot of her just as she turned and looked toward her building. Knowing there wouldn't be a better opportunity, I snapped the picture and made it back in the car just as the doors started to close.

I was almost cradling the phone by the time we stopped at Ditmars Boulevard. I couldn't wait to upload the picture on my computer. When the train stopped, I walked over to the other end of the car and took a picture of the seat where she had been only a few minutes ago. Both pics looked great on the phone. I took the next W back to Astoria Boulevard and took a picture of her building from the platform. The people who saw me probably thought I was taking a picture of the Bridge, so they never even gave me a second thought. It was still too light to get a closer shot of her apartment, so that one would have to wait. Rather than go home and have to come back, I went to Nemo's Diner just under the station, opposite Hoyt

Park. I asked for a booth by the window so I could see her building across from the basketball courts.

As the hostess took me to a booth, someone called out my name. When I turned around, Steve waved at me and motioned me over. He was sitting at a table across from the booth I wanted. I walked over and shook his hand. "Everest, this is my wife, Melissa." He introduced me to a very pretty young woman dressed in a black suit with deep blue eyes. "Hi, nice to meet you," I said. She smiled and nodded.

"Twice in a month's time. What a small world. Honey, this is the friend I told you that I bumped into the other day on the train."

"Oh," she said, still smiling.

"Yeah, small world," I repeated.

"What brings you around here? I've never seen you here before."

"Oh, I come by every so often. Been a while, though."

"We just got here. Neither of us felt like cooking and we live so close to the place, we decided to be lazy tonight."

"Huh, same here. Just being lazy tonight."

"Well, why don't you join us?"

"Oh no, that's ok. I uh…I don't wanna…um, you know, intrude."

"What? Come on! Don't be silly. Pull up a chair."

"No, really, I –" Steve asked the hostess to please bring a chair over and another place setting.

Since I didn't have much of a choice, I sat down. The waiter brought over a menu and I tried to act casual as I looked behind me toward her building, which I could barely make out from where I sat.

"So what do you do?" Melissa asked.

"Huh? Oh, I work in customer service for Astor House Books."

"The bookstore chain."

"Yeah, that's it."

"Wow, I'm in there all the time. Do you work out of a store or…"

"No, I work out of the corporate office downtown."

"Oh really, that's where I am. Where Downtown?" she asked.

"Just off Wall Street. Not too far from Trinity Church."

"I'm on Canal. I work for Sarafega Communications. It's a small internet company."

The waiter finally took our orders and there was a kind of suicidal lull at the table. I was starting to sweat from wanting to turn around and look out the window. "So Everest, are you married?" she asked.

"Honey…" Steve said, almost warning her.

"What? It's a simple question."

"Tell her you're married Everest. Otherwise she's gonna set you up with every single one of her husband-hunting friends."

"Oh I will not! Why, are you looking for someone?" she asked. I smiled at her joke and used the opportunity to sneak another glance over at the building.

I have to say that Steve and his wife were the neatest diners I've ever seen in my whole life. He had the filet of sole with vegetables and Melissa had shrimp scampi over brown rice. There wasn't a small bone or grain of rice that fell off their plate. Discreet bites and they never spoke with their mouths full. Hell, you could barely tell that they were chewing. I had the meatloaf and mashed potatoes and I managed to spill some gravy and roll a green pea or two on the table.

After dinner, Steve and I chatted over old times and talked about people we hadn't seen in years. Melissa sat and listened attentively to the times that Steve was caught sneaking into the girl's locker room and when he turned the teacher's desk drawers upside down and when he slipped a frog scheduled for dissection into Elaine Ramos' purse. "Good times," he said, "different times."

"Sounds like my husband was quite the little hell raiser."

"Nah, he was ok. It was just kid stuff, you know?" I said.

"And what about you, Everest? No stories? I suppose you were just a perfect angel," she said.

"Everest? No, he hung out with us sometimes, but he mostly stayed out of that kind of shit. He only transferred to school during...senior year, was it?"

"Ah, junior year. Middle of junior year, actually."

"Right, so he didn't really know too many people. Kind of shy," he said.

"Silent type," she smiled.

"Besides, these guys were always doing something funny. You didn't want to miss out on whatever they were up to next," I said.

"Remember when Gloria March had the hots for you, man?"

"What?"

"You remember Gloria? She was that band chick with black hair and lots of dandruff? Kind of dumpy looking and wore glasses?"

"I remember Gloria."

"What happened with her?" asked Melissa.

"Nothing happened with her. She just didn't really fit in anywhere. Anyway, I saw her at the reunion and…you remember, honey, she was the one I pointed out to you. The one who was on the cover of *Forbes* a couple of months ago."

"The one who started her own publishing company, yes, I remember her now."

"Everest, you should've seen her. I'll tell you, there're no flakes on her now. She looks fantastic."

As much I enjoyed going over old times, I really wasn't paying much attention to what they were talking about. All I did was check to see if it was dark enough for me to be able to slip into the alleyway and maybe get a picture of her window as soon as we were done. "So Everest, do you live nearby?" The streetlights outside had just come on, so I knew it was getting close. I'd be able to get over there and maybe even catch her looking out the window. To be able to catch her looking at the sky or maybe the Triborough all lit up, the reflection on her window getting her in just the right light.

"Everest?" he asked. I looked up at both of them and realized that I had drifted off for a second. "Huh? I'm sorry, what was that?"

"I just asked if you lived close by," she snuck a puzzling glance over at Steve.

"Oh, uh...not too far, really. I just gotta um, hop on the uh...the bus."

"The bus? Where to?" he asked.

"Ravenswood."

"Ravenswood?" They looked at each other and for the first time ever, I felt kind of embarrassed. It was kind of the way I guess I would feel if I were to tell Elsa that I lived in Ravenswood. "Yeah. It's not so bad, really. The part that I live in isn't too deep in Ravenswood. As a matter of fact, you could hardly call it Ravenswood, really. It's only just past the bridge."

Dessert came, but I only asked for a coffee. Steve and Melissa shared a slice of chocolate cake. They kept giving each other these sly looks now and then, accompanied by a tiny smirk. Apparently there was some sort of inside story about chocolate cake as I remembered Steve smiling slightly when he ordered it while Melissa tucked in her chin and looked at the table. I remember feeling a little envious of the two of them at that moment. It was nice that they had those kinds of secrets, couple secrets. Little things that are meaningless to the rest of the world but have their own significance to the both of you. I'd love to have that. I'd love to have that with Elsa.

After the check was paid, they asked me if I was going straight home. "Um, yeah. Probably."

"Well, you're welcome to come over for a drink at our place, if you like. We're only just a couple of blocks away."

"Oh, no. No, thank you. No, I'm just…gonna get going."

"Aw, come on man, it's early. It's only just 8 now," Steve pressed.

"No, really. Thanks, though, but I'm kind of tired. I think I'm just gonna head on home."

"Ok. Well, maybe some other time, then."

"Sure."

"Well, it was nice meeting you, Everest."

"Thanks. It was nice meeting you, too."

"Take it easy, man. Sorry you're not gonna join us. Gimme a call,

though, ok? We'll set something up for another time."

"Will do. Thanks, again."

I walked up the stairs to the station as if I were going to catch the

train and stayed to watch them as they crossed the street. They

walked down the block, their arms behind one another, holding each

other close. It was as if they were oblivious to the rest of the world

around them. The traffic that swept by, the kids in the park, they

didn't seem to take notice of any of it. They seemed to only hear

what the other was saying. Maybe they were talking about the

whole thing with the chocolate cake, maybe they were making plans

for what they would do later. It was something between them,

something that they had apart from the all the noise outside their

walls. Something that all that bullshit couldn't touch. Just before

they got too far out of range, I took a picture.

I wandered around the neighborhood for a while, waiting for it to get darker. While I waited, I thought about Steve and school and the day I moved to Astoria from Jersey. It was four years after my mother killed herself when we moved and I remember we stopped at the cemetery before going to our new apartment. My mother's cousin bought flowers so I could put them by the headstone and we stood there in silence for a few minutes. He was a good man, but he didn't know what to say and neither did I. That was usually the way it was growing up with him. He would come home from work, he would ask me how school was, I'd say fine, we'd eat, watch TV and go to sleep. He never talked about my mother and I never brought her up. As soon as I was able to, I moved out and started working. We kept in touch occasionally until he died in a car accident about ten years ago.

I didn't stray too far from her block, but I also didn't stick around too closely. I did manage to see a few people walk in and out of her building, nobody that I recognized from the other times, though. At around 10:30 I figured it was late enough to be able to get down the alley, so I came up from the other direction, looked to see if there was maybe another way to get there instead of from the front like before. That way, I'd cut my chances of being spotted by someone.

On the block that was on the other side of Elsa's there were a string of conjoined, two family houses. Directly behind these houses was a long strip of driveway that stretched from one end of the block to the other, which was separated from the buildings on Elsa's block by a large concrete wall. This driveway was for the tenants of those houses to get to their private parking spots behind their homes. They got to it through an entrance from either end, which is Astoria Boulevard or the other side, 24th Avenue. Ducking down the driveway from 24th Avenue, I walked to the other side until I got to where I could see the top of her building. Luckily, the driveway only had three overhead lights for the whole stretch, two of which were out, so I didn't think that anyone could really see me.

Scaling the wall wasn't easy. I was never much of an athlete, but I managed to get up and over without causing myself any damage. I hid in the shadows of the garbage cans until I got my bearings.

From there I saw her window. Her light was on and just above the windows I saw gray clouds, storm clouds. The wind seemed to pick up a little, but it felt good. If anything, it blew the stink of the garbage away from me.

After what felt like hours, I looked at my watch. It was 11:30 already. I had totally lost track of time again. There were only a few lights on in her building. Suddenly, the light in her room went out but a few moments later, I saw down the alley that she had turned one on in another room. For a while, I just stared at the window on the side of the building. Her window. What could she be doing? I was sure that someone like her had much more of an interesting social life than one that could find her home on a Friday night. "Maybe she's not alone," I wondered out loud.

The next thing I knew, I was standing underneath the fire escape, which led to her bedroom window. There was nobody around and the other apartments had turned their lights off. I started to actually consider climbing up and taking a peek inside. That wouldn't be so bad, would it? I mean, it wasn't like I was going to catch her getting dressed or in the bathroom or anything. I just wanted to see what her apartment looked like. Besides, I figured that that would probably be the only way that I would ever find out how she lived. Maybe she would have some frames on a dresser or on the wall, people in her life that she thought about. People just like her. I started to remember how I had pictured her room in my fantasy and the next thing I knew, I was hanging from the bottom rung of the fire escape ladder.

Luckily for me, everybody on the first and second floors had their shades drawn and there was no light that would cast a shadow walking past their window so my only concern was trying to be as quiet as I could while I climbed. My heart was beating so hard, I couldn't hear anything else around me. All I got was this pounding in my ears and the sound of my own breathing. When I finally got to the third floor, I saw that the top portion of the window was about halfway open. I crouched down and looked inside. The room was totally dark and it took a minute for me to make out the figures inside. A small nightstand with an alarm clock and cordless phone stood next to a Queen-size bed on the left, right in the middle of the wall. The bed had a white comforter and two large, white pillows by the headboard. Next to the window on my left, was a chestnut brown dresser. I could see that there were some frames on top, but they were turned toward the door so I couldn't see the images. The open door was right in front of me and a fairly large, white closet door was to the right. There was a carpet on the floor and the walls were painted a modest white.

Just past the door was a semi-lit hallway leading to a larger room that had the light on. I felt a few drops hit me and looked up to see that the sky had been completely covered in gray clouds. I turned up my collar. When I squinted slightly, I saw a foot hanging off of what looked like the arm of a brown leather couch. The TV was flashing in front of it and the foot slowly started to swing from side to side. I don't remember if there was anything else beyond that room. Truth of the matter was that I didn't look. All I could see was that foot. That delicate little foot, gently moving as if to keep up with some rhythm. The rain was starting to come down a little harder and I felt the water start to run down the back of my neck and into my shirt. Even though I was scared to move, scared to do anything that could even slightly disturb the scene, I took out my phone.

There was a bright flash of white for a second and I nearly fell on my ass when I saw my own shadow laid out across her bedroom floor before realizing that was just some lightning. A loud rumble followed and I steadied myself against the building. The rain started to come down harder. Then I realized that the storm could work to my advantage. With the lightning, my camera flash wouldn't look like anything more than just another streak. It was perfect! When I peered inside again, I saw that the foot hadn't stopped moving.

To think that she was just a few feet away from me, on a Friday night yet! Somebody like her lounging around her apartment, moving her foot to the sounds of the TV that I was barely able to make out. My erection was straining against my wet jeans and I tried not to think about it. Still, sitting outside her window, thinking about how she might look relaxing on the couch didn't make it easy. She was probably bored with whatever was on, wondering what her friends were doing and if she should have reconsidered going out with them. After all, she had worked hard all week, why shouldn't she go out there and have some fun? She was entitled. She deserved it. I couldn't stop staring at her foot.

Another blinding flash of lightning reminded me that I had better hurry and get the picture before I got busted creeping around on someone's fire escape. I looked at my screen and snapped a quick shot just as the foot suddenly stopped moving. Just in case that didn't come out, I took another one. I don't think she noticed the flash going off. There was no reason to pay attention to it anyway, in that type of weather. After I checked the shot in the camera, I smiled when I saw how perfect it had come out. Her foot captured perfectly in that one instant. God, it was perfect.

It really started to pour. I saw the foot disappear and the TV stopped flashing. Figuring that she was probably shutting everything off and heading in my direction, I hurried down the fire escape, almost slipped on the steps, and was able to climb down the ladder and hide behind the garbage cans again before I saw her turn on her bedroom light.   I looked down the side of the building and up at her floor and saw that she had turned everything off. It looked as if she was getting ready for bed. Then I saw her. She closed the window and stared up at the sky for a few seconds. If it was at all possible, she looked better than she did on the train. She wore a gray, short-sleeve sweatshirt and ran her fingers through her short, blonde hair. While I wasn't able to see their color, I saw that she had almond-shaped eyes. Elsa. Elsa Graham. I kept repeating her name over and over again. That would have been a perfect shot. Watching her look up at the storm, that perfect face, that perfect body standing there. I reached for the phone before realizing that she might notice some "lightning" coming from below her window. Putting it back in my pocket, I looked up and saw her turn away from the window. A few minutes later, the light went off.

The rest of the building seemed asleep as well. Rain and a few bursts of lightning and thunder notwithstanding, it seemed to me like all of Astoria was asleep. Everyone but me. I was on my knees, surrounded by garbage in the pouring rain. I kept thinking about the way she looked at the window just a moment ago. The way her foot kept wagging over the arm of the couch. I remember thinking that she probably looked like an angel when she was sleeping. Taking one last, quick look around to make sure that nobody was looking at me, I decided to find out.

I jumped up to grab the last rung on the ladder and hung there for a few seconds. The rain against my face was actually felt pretty good. Even though my clothes were stuck to my body, I barely noticed just how soaked I really was. I pulled myself up and reached for the second rung. It seemed harder to do the second time around. When I finally got a hold of it, I rested for a second and then reached up with my other hand. My legs were swinging underneath me, trying to get a firm place to stand on. It wasn't until I got to the third rung that my right leg was able to reach the first one. I steadied myself and shook the water out of my eyes. Her window was dark, but luckily, she hadn't drawn the curtains. I imagined what she looked like, lying there under silk sheets, her blonde hair slightly undone but still framing her face perfectly, dreaming about who knows what. She had to look like an angel. I knew that she had to.

My leg pushed me up and I reached for the next bar. When I placed my left foot on the second rung, though, it slipped because it was so wet and I banged my head against the side of the ladder. I lost my grip, landed flat on my back and hit the back of my head on the concrete.

Luckily, I didn't black out, but I knew better than to just sit up right away. I checked the back of my head, and while there was no blood, when I touched my forehead though, I felt a small cut which left some blood on my fingers. After I looked around to make sure that I wasn't being watched, I got up slowly and glanced up at her window. Still dark. She was totally clueless as to what had happened just underneath her window. At least, I hoped she was. My body ached and the rain would not let up, so I thought it would be a good idea if I cut my losses and called it a night. The way I saw it, I was damned lucky that I hadn't killed myself in that fall. Granted, it was only about 8' or so, but still, I could've landed on my head or broken something. I was able to walk away with a little cut on my forehead. Besides, at least I was able to see her, and that's what was important to me. I saw her apartment, I saw her in her apartment. Nothing else mattered. Not even the rain or the blood or the garbage.

Chapter Twelve

It was tough getting home. I felt like shit. Finally, after about two blocks I gave up and got in a cab. The driver kept looking at me in the mirror and asked me if I was okay. "You want go to hospeetal?"

"No. No, I'm okay. Just get me home."

"You sure? Hospeetal close. Few blocks."

"No. Just...home. Thank you." He shrugged his shoulders and muttered something. My cut was still bleeding and I had to wipe some out of my left eye. It was still raining hard. During the ride, I grabbed the phone and checked to make sure I hadn't somehow broken the damn thing in the fall, it seemed fine. I quickly checked the pictures, they were still there. Traffic was pretty steady, there really weren't any people out. I had heard some people in the projects, mostly Hilda, say that they prefer it when it rains. The water seems to wash everything away, but I think they were just talking about the way that it kept certain people away. Although, I never really saw any difference. The projects still looked like the projects. The only difference was that the garbage lying in the street was wet garbage.

"Hey…miztur. You need help?" he asked. He seemed pretty sincere about it, but I didn't take him up on his offer. Instead, I tipped him and staggered out until I got my bearings and made my way past the courtyard and into my building. When I walked in, Simone was just getting back from throwing out the garbage. "Oh my Gaw, wha' happen' to you?"

"Huh? Nothing. I uh, I just got caught in the rain, that's all."

"Jesus, you bleedin'!"

"Oh, yeah. I…fell…while I was out. Banged my head."

"You awright?"

"Yeah. Thanks." Just then I sneezed suddenly and felt kind of woozy. I swayed a bit and Simone came and tried to steady me. "Whoa. Lissen, I don' think dat you ok. You shuh proly go to a hospital."

"I don't need to go to a hospital. Why does everyone keep sayin' that?" I remember leaning against the wall at that moment. If that hadn't been there, I would probably have been on the floor.

"Come awn, why doncha come inside? Rest up a bit."

"No. I just…I just want to go home."

"You shua?"

"Yeah. Yeah, I'm fine, thanks. I'll be okay once I get home."

"You ga somebody upstairs? Help you out?"

"Yeah," I lied, without knowing why. "Listen, thanks, really. I'll be okay. Like I said, I just want to…go home."

"Ok. Here, lemme get da elevatuh for ya." So she walked me to the damn elevator. When we got to the end of the hallway, some guy dressed in black walked in through the front and stood at Simone's door. "Be right dair!" she called out. "Lissen, you shua you gonna be ok?" She pushed the up button. "I'll be fine. Go ahead, really. Thanks again." The door slid open just then and after I got inside, I saw her walk toward the guy in black. She kissed him on the cheek and in they went.

As soon as I finished getting cleaned up in the bathroom and cursing the shit out of the fucking anti-septic and the fire escape and the goddamn bump on the back of my head, I sat in front of my computer and uploaded the pictures. Each of them came out perfectly. Especially the one where she was walking toward the stairs on the station and the one with her foot over the sofa. There were others surrounding her in the picture where she was walking

away, but she outshined all of them. She was dead center in the

middle of a lot of gray and dull black, but she didn't blend in or got

lost in any of it. Then there was that naked foot. While I stared at

the picture I totally forgot about the pain in my back. All I could

focus on was watching her, memorizing every detail of that naked

foot and imagining what it would be like to…touch it.

In my mind, I was massaging the bottom of that foot, staring at

first at the bright red polish on the nails and then following my

fingers as they glided along the side and to the top of the ankle. The

T.V. would be on mute and she would smile as I lightly tickled her.

Every once in a while, the lightning would flash and then her other

foot would move against my leg. Her arms would be up over her

head and she'd stretch as she gently pushed me away with her foot

over the edge. The power would go out suddenly and we were both

startled at first. She'd give me a little smile that told me she wanted

to play. As I'd sit down next to her, feeling her long and lean body

underneath her sweats, she'd know I was ready. Another flash of

lighting and she'd take her top off, letting my hands fall on her breasts as she reached up to pull me closer. The wind would blow the curtains in and as we'd collapse on the floor, tearing at each other's clothes. We'd feel drops of rain on our skin, but it wouldn't matter and we wouldn't care. If the roof caved in suddenly, we'd probably barely noticed. She would be on top of me quickly and my hands would move with her hips while she rocked her back and forth, calling and listening to our names and groans while the lightning gave us peeks at each other every time it flashed white.

The phone rang and fucked the whole thing up. I opened my eyes and realized that I had been jerking off again. Her foot was still up on the screen and my hand relaxed around the base of my hard-on. The phone rang again and this sickening feeling came over me that I only usually get in the morning. It was a mixture of nausea, coldness, and that feeling you get after the initial sting of getting kicked in the groin. After the third ring, the answering machine picked up. After the beep, I heard the familiar voice call out. Pulling up my sweats, I answered the phone. "Yo! Wassup dude?! Where you been, yo?" he said.

"Hello?" I asked.

"Hello?"

"HELLO!"

"Yo…yo, who dis?" asked a very confused voice.

"Who's this?! Who's this?!"

"Yo, Sanchez? Dat you, bro?"

"No you fucking asshole! It's not fucking Sanchez, okay?! Sanchez doesn't fucking live here. He's never lived here! OKAY?! You got that?! Can you possibly compre-fucking-hend that little fact or is it too much for your pea brain to handle?!"

"Yo…who – "

"Want me to spell it out for you? Ok, I'll spell it out for you. SANCHEZ DOESN'T FUCKING LIVE HERE ASSHOLE!! HOW 'BOUT THAT?! YOU GOT IT YOU FUCKING LOW-LIFE PIECE OF SHIT?!"

"Yo fuck you, man! Fuck you, you fucking faggot!!"

"No, FUCK YOU! FUCK YOU! FUCK YOU! FUCK YOU UNTIL YOU DIE YOU ROTTEN, NO-GOOD FILTHY SCUMBAG, PIECE OF SHIT! FUCK YOU!!" Before he could answer, I ripped the cord out of the jack and threw the phone against the wall, getting a kind of cool chill when I saw it smash open.

There was this kind of eerie quiet afterward. The only thing I could hear besides the rain tapping on the window was my heartbeat. It felt like it was going to burst out of my chest again. I looked over at my computer and the screen saver had already kicked in. My erection was gone, naturally, so I thought that rather than start it up again, I'd just shut down the computer and go to bed. Besides, my head started to hurt.

While in my bed in the dark, I started to think about everything that happened. I had to lie on my side because the bump on the back of my head would hurt when I was on the pillow. Even though I was in pain, I still thought it was worth it. She was home. She was just lounging around her apartment in some sweats, watching TV and going to bed early. I would've loved to have seen her sleeping just then. Right before I drifted off to sleep, I remember thinking that maybe the next time, I would.

I spent most of the weekend staring at the pictures. My body still ached from Friday night, so I just took it easy and popped some

Tylenol. After I played with them on Photoshop where I changed the sizes and colors, I printed them so I could put them on the wall next to my computer. Even though I still hurt, I felt pretty good so I put on some music through Pandora. Elvis Costello's *I Want You* came on and I made some iced tea while I decided how to arrange her pictures on the wall. Hilda had asked me to dog sit Cherry the night before, so she sat on the couch and watched as I laid out the pictures on my desk. "What do you think, should I put this one up next or this one?" I asked her, holding a picture of Elsa from the train platform that I had changed to black and white, and a picture of her bedroom window that I had made larger. She looked at me and quizzically tilted her head. "You're right, why not both? They're going to wind up there anyway," I said, and taped them next to each other on the wall.

After I walked and fed Cherry, I took her back to Hilda's.

"Thanks so much for watching her."

"No problem."

"You feeling better?" she asked, motioning to the band aid on my head.

"Yeah, thanks, I'm fine. How are you doing?"

"Did you see a doctor?"

"No, really I'm fine. It's nothing. Just a little gash, that's all. How are you?"

"I'm okay. As okay as can be expected when you're my age. Don't get old, Everest, that's all I can say."

"I'll keep that in mind, Hilda."

"Still, sometimes I look at my children and my grandchildren and I'm grateful that I've lived this long to see them, you know? Not everybody is as lucky. My sister, she died when she was only twenty-one years old. Can you believe that?"

"Wow, that's terrible," I said.

"And on the night she got engaged!"

"Really?"

"Mm-hm. She went out for a ride with her fiancé and they got into a terrible car crash. He lost a leg and she died right there on the spot."

"God, I'm sorry Hilda."

"Course I was only a child when it happened, but I remember it like it was yesterday. My mother, it broke her heart. And my father, he was never the same man after that. Something like that, it changes you, you know? You don't ever look at things the same way again after something like that."

"Yeah, that's true."

"That's why you have to try to enjoy every minute you're above ground, baby. Take those chances today because you never know what's going to happen tomorrow."

"You're so right," I said, remembering Friday night.

"Well, you go get some rest, baby. If you need anything, let me know."

"Thanks Hilda, I will."

When I was back in my apartment, I turned on the television and tried to forget about the pictures and the phone and the pain in my back. That conversation with Hilda reminded me of the time my mom took me to her father's funeral. I was around nine years old at the time and had never been to one before, and honestly I didn't really know the man. My mom never really said much about him only that it was very lonely growing up with him since her mother had died when she was very young. She did mention that he was very affectionate, but seemed to change the subject quickly whenever I asked her to tell me more about her childhood. On the cab ride to the funeral, I noticed that she seemed to get more and more nervous the closer we got. She kept ringing her hands together and once we got out of the cab, she held onto mine tighter than I ever remember. As we made our way through the parlor, I noticed people in the room would quickly look at her, then at me and look away. She didn't say a word to anyone, but walked me right up to the casket.

He was dressed in a plain gray suit with a black tie and had rosary beads wrapped around his folded hands. I heard my mother whisper something, but I couldn't make out what it was. She looked at him, drew in a deep breath and leaned on the casket slightly. A tear welled up in her eye and slowly made its way down her cheek, eventually falling from her face and landing on the back of my hand. I looked at him, but didn't feel the urge to cry and I began to wonder if there was something wrong with me. Obviously, my mom was upset about this, but I couldn't feel anything about what had happened. He was a stranger to me. After a few minutes, we turned around and walked out, never having said a single word to anyone there.

I had only seen him once before then. He came by our apartment a couple of years before that as a surprise. Looking back, my mom seemed more unsettled than pleased by his visit. They spoke, briefly, at the door before she finally let him in and he wound up introducing himself to me as my grandfather. He handed me a wrapped box and said it was a present. I looked at my mom and she stared at the box, nodding that it was ok for me to open. Inside, there was a brand new baseball and baseball glove. Nobody had ever given me a present like that before and I wasn't really into baseball, but I remember feeling happy just getting something like that. He smiled when I thanked him and then he and my mom stepped into the kitchen for the rest of his visit. After a while, I heard them start to argue and went to see what was happening. I saw my mom slam the refrigerator door close and yell at him to get out. Without another word, he stood up, looked at me for a second and then quietly walked out the door. My mother shut the locks quickly, told me to watch some TV and then spent the rest of the day in her room.

Later on, I started to zone out during a re-run of *Friends*. When a commercial for some skin cream came on, the woman splashing water on her face looked like Elsa. The water was falling away from her hands and face in slow motion and her eyes were closed. The narrator rattled off some bullshit about the cream and Elsa slowly looked right at me. Her pale blue eyes really stood out from the white walls and furniture that surrounded her. She wore a white tee shirt and white pants and the camera kept panning around her, but she never lost contact with me. They cut away to show the bottle the cream came in and then they showed her rubbing some on her face. I got upset every time they cut away, which they seemed to be doing a lot to show some computer graphic of the way the cream penetrates and moisturizes the skin. I mean, who gave a fuck?! The commercial was trying to make it seem as if using the cream would make other women look like Elsa. Who the hell were they kidding?! As if Elsa needed that shit to begin with! When they finally cut back to her, she was smiling at the camera. It wasn't until the end of the commercial when she spoke, that I realized that it wasn't her. The voice was different, deeper and when I really looked at her, I noticed that the woman in the commercial seemed a little heavier than Elsa around the cheeks. When *Friends* came back, I turned off the TV and flipped on my computer.

Chapter Thirteen

I didn't see her on the train on Monday. Tuesday was a no-show too. I was thinking about going back to her building again when I realized that some asshole from Alabama was babbling in my ear about how offended she was that the *Sports Illustrated Swimsuit* issue was on display in one of our stores. It was Wednesday, 11:57. I still had a while to go before I could leave. After her rant, she quoted a bible passage and hung up.

Floyd was already in the pizzeria when I showed up. He smiled and motioned me to join him. Although I really wasn't in the mood, I sat down anyway and nodded while he smiled at me. "Haven't ssseen you inna while, Everest."

"I know. Guess you forgot your sandwich again today, huh?"

"Yeah, I dddid. Funny huh?"

"Million laughs."

"Did you have a good weekend? Wwwhat happened to your head?"

"Oh, it's nothing. Just a little accident I had, that's all. Yeah, I had a good weekend, thanks."

"Oh. I had a gggood weekend too. I wwwent to this pool hall near my house."

"Sounds like fun," I said, taking a bite of the cheese slice.

"Yeah. Hey, how's it gggoing with Brian? I heard he's llleaving."

"Yeah, his last day is coming up next week. Word gets around, huh?"

"Sure does. I heard he got a better offer somewhere."

"Really? I wouldn't know."

"Hasn't he said anything?"

"I don't know, Floyd. I don't really hang out with anybody from work, you know? If Brian got a better job somewhere else, good for him. At least he won't have to deal with stupid people on the phone all day."

"Yeah, good for him," he agreed, looking a little surprised by my reaction. Really though, what else was I supposed to say? He was obviously fishing for office gossip and there wasn't any to give.

I saw a couple of other people from the office come in to buy some pizza. None of them stayed, though. On days when it's sunny out, most of them will eat at the park by City Hall. "Have they hired

somebody to fffill in for Brian?"

"Yeah. He's some Assistant Manager in a store out in Long Island."

"Have you met him?"

"No. George already interviewed him though." When we finished

lunch and walked out of the place, it looked like Floyd wanted to tag

along while I walked around. As I tried to think of a way to put the

idea out of his head, I saw a woman with a cat sitting on the

sidewalk against our building. Her face was dirty, almost as black as

the clothes she wore, and right by her torn Keds sneakers, she had a

cardboard sign that read, "Please help my kitty and me. Hungry,

HIV+ and homeless. God bless. Thank you." She had a little paper

cup next to the sign with a dollar and some change in it. Before we

reached the corner, I turned and looked at her again, watching as

people ignored her and went about their business. Suddenly, I

remembered Elsa and that time she gave Ben that

sandwich on the train. "Floyd, you go on ahead, I gotta do

something."

"Is everything ok?"

"Yeah, it's fine. I'll see you back at the office," and without waiting for him to respond, I turned around and went back to the pizzeria. I bought a slice, some garlic knots and a medium Coke. I stuck my head out to see if Floyd had left and as I watched him wobble down the street, I walked up to the woman. She slowly lifted her head and squinted slightly from the glare of the sun. The kitty looked up at me as well, as if it were waiting for me to say something. I just stood there, holding the bag and Coke. She had blue eyes. It was a different kind of blue, though. As if they needed more color. They weren't bright, they was more of a dull blue; kind of like faded jeans.

"Um, I…uh…are you…hungry?" I mumbled. She nodded and looked at the bag. I handed it to her and gave her the Coke. "It's uh…it's a slice and some garlic knots. I don't know if you like…garlic knots. Or pizza."

"Thanks."

"You're welcome. Sorry, I didn't get anything for uh…for the uh…your kitty."

"Okay. That's okay. Thanks again. God bless you, sir." She took a sip of the soda and opened the bag. I stood there watching her while she pulled out the slice and fished around for the garlic knots. She looked up at me and smiled. "God bless you," she said, her mouth full. I don't remember if I smiled, but I bent down to pet the kitty.

When I got back to my cube, I was having a hard time focusing on work. I kept thinking of the woman sitting right outside the building and how much she really seemed to enjoy that slice. Who knows when the last time was that she had a hot meal? Who knows when she'll have one again? At least I was helped out, even if it was for just one slice. "Hey, what's with the grin?" Brian said. He was trying to hand me something. "Hmm? Oh, nothing. Uh, what's up?"

"Annual blood drive announcement. They really are trying to squeeze out every drop from you."

"You giving?"

"I'm almost outta here, man. There's no way that they're getting anymore out of me than I've already given them." I read over the paper and almost threw it away. Just as I was about to add it to the pile of crumbled up balls in my wastebasket, I thought about Elsa.

She would definitely be the type to give blood. The chance to save someone's life? That's definitely her style. For God's sake, she gave a big smelly guy on the train some food of course she'd give some of her blood in a nice, sterile environment. I remembered how good it felt just to give that woman a slice of pizza and I made up my mind to donate. I tacked it up on my board so I wouldn't forget.

The train stalled on my way home. We were parked between the 23rd and 28th Street stations for 10 goddamn deadly minutes. I closed my eyes so as not to have to look at everyone but little by little, I kept sneaking a peek. I couldn't help it, it was like trying not to look at a car accident. All those people had the same mangled look on their face, you know? The same look across the board. It's that look you got at the end of the day, whether or not you had a rough one.

We finally pulled into Lexington Avenue, but she didn't get on. When I got off at Ditmars, I started to walk towards the bus stop, but I turned around and instead walked the other way, back toward her neighborhood. Hell, it was only a few blocks away. Without realizing it, I felt the phone in my pocket as I got closer. When I got to the corner of her block, I saw her across the street as she went into the grocery store. I started to wonder if she had noticed that I wasn't on the train today. Did she even remember me at all? It was probably too much to hope for.

The next thing I knew, I was in front of the store. It kind of spooked me at first because I didn't even remember crossing the street. I stood right at the door, watching her pay for some things and taking the paper bag the pudgy old guy behind the counter gave her. Suddenly, the door swung open and she walked out.

We were face to face. The whole world seemed to stop at that second when it was just me and her. She had apparently changed out of her suit and into the sweats that I saw her wearing the other night. She gasped slightly as she stopped short of running into me. God that would've been great. Maybe she would've dropped her bag and I would've caught it just in time before it touched the ground. Of course, she would smile and ask me if we hadn't met somewhere before. Did she remember? It hadn't too long ago that we spoke at the train station, she had to remember. She wasn't the type that forgot people. Especially if it was someone who had made a complete ass of himself just trying to hand her back a dry cleaning ticket. I caught my reflection in her Ray Bans and saw the bandage on my forehead. Maybe she *would* remember. Maybe she would remember and ask me what happened. I'd have to think of something to say. After all, I couldn't very well tell her that I banged my head while I was trying to sneak up her fire escape. I was getting frantic while trying to think of something to say, some bullshit explanation. Instead, she just gripped the bag a little more tightly and smirked as she said, "Oh…sorry," while she squeezed past me and hurried herself back across the street.

I watched her until she disappeared from site. She didn't even turn around. I guessed that she hadn't remembered me. Maybe she was in a hurry? That must've been it. She was in a hurry. But in a hurry to do what, I wondered. From what I saw, she lived alone. At least, she seemed to live alone. I never saw her with anybody so it wasn't like she needed to get home and start dinner for someone or something like that. Maybe she was expecting a phone call? It must've been a pretty important phone call if she couldn't even stop and say hello to the guy who got crushed trying to return something she dropped.

"Excuse me, Mister?" a little voice sang. I looked down and there was this little blonde girl looking up at me with these big green eyes. "What?" I asked.

"I just want to get through," she answered and I realized that I was blocking her way. I walked out into the street and soon found myself at the park, staring at her building. I knew that I was making too much of things. So she didn't say hello, so what? So she didn't recognize me, big deal. Why the hell should she? Who the hell was I that she should remember me? Just some guy standing in her way while she tried to get home and get on with her life.

I made it back to my building, still wondering if she thought about me at all. It was kind of frustrating to realize that I'd spent all this time thinking about her and she hadn't even given me a second thought. While I don't fool myself into thinking that I'm the model type, I don't think that I'm that bad either. Before going inside, I took a look at myself in the glass door leading into the lobby. Aside from the bandage on my forehead, there wasn't anything different from what I normally saw in the mirror. Just under 6', short black hair parted down the left side, clean-shaven. Thin, but not anorexic. Okay, maybe a little pale, but I'm not an Albino. As I reached for the door, though, I caught sight of something. There was something in the face that I hadn't noticed right

away. I took a step closer to get a better look. What the hell was it? The face was the same, but still it had changed slightly. It seemed different to me somehow. I got a little closer. The eyes looked a little darker. Not the eyes themselves, actually, but the whole area. There were dark circles, like I hadn't slept in days. I noticed, too, that I wasn't all that clean-shaven. In fact, I had more than just a five o'clock shadow going on it looked like I hadn't shaved at all in two days. I had that blue-gray color across the lower half of my face. And when the hell had I started to hunch? While I was looking over my face, I realized that my shoulders were practically reaching my ears.

The door opened suddenly and Simone asked if I was going to go inside. I barely registered what she had said. "Huh?" I asked.

"You comin' in? Wha' happen' you fuhget ya keys?"

"Oh. Uh...no. No, I was just ah...um, forget it."

"Faget wha, you aint said nuthin'," she smiled. I noticed that she was missing a tooth on the right bottom row.

"Yeah." I walked past her and tried not to look down her top. I wouldn't normally, except that she was wearing this really tight, black push-up thing. I think they call it a bustier or something. She must've noticed because she smiled and kept looking at me.

"How you feelin'?" she asked, pointing to my forehead with her chin.

"Fine, fine. Thanks. Thank you."

"You see a doctah?"

"Uh, no. No, I'm fine, really. Thanks." I stood in front of my mailbox and fumbled for my key. Why the hell was I so spastic all of a sudden?

"You really should, you know, 'cause dat could be sumthin' serious, you know?"

"Yeah."

"I mean, maybe it don't feel bad now an' all, but it could, like, develop into sumthin' bad. Real bad. I had this fren one time, she um, got into a car accident and she thought that she was okay but she started feelin' worse and worse and the next day, she was dead." I found my key and opened my mailbox. She was standing next to me and I looked at her painted face and took a whiff of whatever the hell perfume she had showered with and for some reason, I thought about Elsa again. I thought about her and how she hadn't even given me the time of day. Then I remembered what I looked like and I kind of rolled my shoulders back and stood up straight. I think I heard something crack.

"That's too bad." I scooped up the junk mail and bills and closed my box. She looked me up and down, leaned in a little closer and said, "Thanks. So lissen, you wanna – "

"Everest, how are you?" I looked over Simone's head and saw Hilda walk through the door. She was leaning on a silver cane and came right up to us, Cherry in tow. I remember I wondered when

the hell she started using a cane. "Hi, Hilda. I'm fine, thanks. How

you doin'?"

"I'm fine. How's your head?"

"I axed him dat and he tol' me dat he's fine but you know how

sumtimes these things don't come atchu for a couple hours."

"How do you feel?" she asked, ignoring Simone.

"I feel fine," I bent down and petted Cherry while she licked my

hand.

"Any headaches?"

"No. I'm fine, really. What about you? Since when did you start

walking with a cane?"

"Oh, about a week now. Remember, I told you that my knee was

starting to act up so this helps me get around."

"Of that's right, forgot," I lied. I had no memory of that

conversation. "Sorry to hear it."

"Yeah, dat's terrible," Simone kept looking at me.

"Well if you need anything, Everest, don't think twice about

asking."

"Thanks, Hilda."

"You going up?" she asked. Simone threw her a sharp look.

"Yeah. Nice talking to you, Simone."

"A pleasure," she answered. I walked with Hilda to the elevator and as I held the door open, I caught Simone staring at us.

"So how're things going with your lady friend?" she asked as we rode up. Just then I felt my cut itch. "My lady friend?"

"The one that had you all smiles the other day. Don't tell me that was Simone."

"Huh? Oh, no! Her name's Elsa. She's…good. I actually saw her recently."

"That's good."

"Yeah, I thought I'd take her to dinner this weekend."

"Where are you thinking of taking her?"

"I don't know yet." The door opened on her floor and she slowly walked out. Cherry sat and waited while she turned around to talk to me.

"Well, what does she like to eat?" I thought about her question and started to wonder why I had told her I was going to have dinner with

Elsa. Even though, none of that had happened, I kept going with the story.

"Italian," I said.

"There's this really nice place over on Ditmars that you should take her to, then. It's called L'Incontro. My kids take me there sometimes, it's my favorite place."

"That works out really well actually because she lives on that side of Astoria."

"There you go."

"Thanks Hilda. Talk to you soon."

"Let me know how it goes," she said as I let the elevator door close.

The rest of the night was rough. I had the T.V. on, but couldn't concentrate on anything. It was kind of hard to focus on whatever bullshit they had on when she was the only thing that ran through my mind. I sat in front of my desktop and stared at the pictures of her I had saved as the wallpaper and the prints I had taped to the wall. There was one where I caught her profile as she walked away from me at the Astoria Boulevard station. I started to wonder what she was doing just then. What was she doing that she had to rush off

from the grocery store? What kind of life did she lead? Was it all
that different from mine? Of course it was, it had to be. It had to be
different from mine and the grocery store guy and Hilda and Steve
and Captain Marvel and everyone else. She was kind and caring and
not at all selfish. I mean, she gave a homeless guy some food and
then there was that conversation with her fat friend on the train that
time. Was it possible that it was all just a fluke? Was it possible
that maybe I just caught her on a couple of good days? It couldn't
be. "It better not be," I heard myself say.

Chapter Fourteen

I called out sick the next day. I left George some lame message on his voice mail that I had been up all night on the toilet, which was always a sure fire way to get out of work. Besides, I didn't even remember the last time I had called out sick. It was 5:30 in the morning after I left the message. I figured getting up at that hour would give me enough time to get dressed and get to her building before she left for work. Having put on a pair of dark jeans, a black shirt and gray hoodie, I figured I was well hidden enough to venture out.

Rather than wait for the bus and all that shit, I took a cab and told the driver to drop me off at Hoyt Park. The park was empty, but Nemo's across the street was pretty busy. Traffic had just started to build up. 6:10 in the morning and already the Triborough was congested. It was mostly construction vehicles carrying equipment and blue-collar guys to sweat it out for the next 8 hours. There were a few people that walked toward the station, suits, jeans and paint-splattered overalls alike. At five minutes to 7, Elsa walked out of her building. She looked beautiful. Barely 7 and already, she was amazing. She wore a light gray suit with a sky-blue blouse. The early morning wind just sort of teased her hair. She almost seemed to tower above everybody that she passed by.

As she reached the corner to cross the street, I saw another familiar face just a few paces behind. Steve was talking on his cell phone and was walking toward the station in his double-breasted, advertising armor. I froze. What the hell was I supposed to do? It was one thing to follow someone and keep out of sight, but trying to hide from two people, including one that I knew from high school? I was a Customer Service rep, not James Bond.

I walked away from the sidewalk, further into the park. There was a bench nearby that I crouched behind and pretended I was tying my shoelaces. I watched everyone get to the stairs and saw Elsa walk up with Steve almost right behind her. I stood up and casually walked up the steps, cursing Steve out in my mind for blocking my view and fucking everything up. He was three people ahead of me and when we got to the top, the person walking behind him almost bumped into him when his Metro card didn't scan through the turnstile correctly. When he turned around to apologize, I thought he would catch me, but he hadn't stopped talking on his cell phone so he didn't notice.

I decided it would be too risky to get caught by Steve, so I came up with an alternative. Instead of following her, I stayed behind to see if I could somehow get into her apartment. She would be at work all day and I would have that whole time to see what kind of person she was and what kind of life she led. I would have full access to her most intimate of secrets. The idea excited me the more I thought about it and so once I made sure that Steve hadn't seen me, I turned around and made my way back to the street.

Since most people left for work during the morning, I waited around the park for a while before walking into her building. After an hour had passed and I saw that only a few people left her building, I thought it was safe to try. Besides, I was so anxious to get inside her apartment I couldn't have waited any longer. As I got closer to her building, however, I started to wonder how I would manage to get inside. Obviously, her door wouldn't be unlocked and there was no way to get inside past the foyer without a key. Then I remembered that she had kept her bedroom window slightly opened the other night when I saw her, so I figured that had to be my only chance.

I did the same thing I had done the last time, which was to go around through the other block and climb the wall. At that hour, I figured most people would have left for work so that minimized my chances of being seen. After I checked the area, I quickly got to her side of the wall. While I crouched by the garbage cans, I looked around, adjusted the hood over my head and when I saw that there wasn't anyone around, I jumped up and climbed up the fire-escape.

In retrospect, it wasn't exactly the most well-thought out plan. I realize now that it looked pretty conspicuous dressed in dark clothes with a hoodie, trying to get into a window from the third floor of a fire-escape. At the time, I wasn't thinking along rational lines, obviously. All I thought about was Elsa. Luckily, although the window was closed all the way, it was unlocked. I slowly opened the window and stepped inside. Crouching by the window, I listened and waited. For what exactly, I wasn't sure, but I thought it would be smart to be still for a minute and get my bearings.

I remember the feeling I had the first time I was actually in her room. It was a mix of excitement, wonder and fear. Each came together in the pit of my stomach and slowly spread throughout my body until they became goose bumps on my skin. Her bedroom was very bright. With the sun streaming in, you wouldn't need to turn on a single light in the whole apartment. Slowly walking across the carpet, I figured I would start at the far end of the apartment and make my way to her bedroom. At the other side of her place was a kind of sitting room. There was a purple area rug in the middle, and two large windows that faced Astoria Boulevard where you were able to see over Hoyt Park and even the train station. There was an antique-looking, floral pattern couch against the wall close by with two satin pillows on the ends. Hanging on the wall above it was a large, black and white print of a ballerina lying down on a wooden bench, overlooking the skyline. On the other side, there was a mini-bar with a few bottles of wine and some other hard liquor.

The living/dining room was next. A dark mahogany, square 5-piece dining room table and chairs were on the left with what looked like a fresh bouquet of yellow tulips in a glass vase in the center. On the other side of the room next to the doorway on the right was an "L-shaped" green micro-fiber couch. Directly opposite that, hanging on the wall was a 60" flat screen TV. For a minute, I stood in the middle of the room and stared at the couch, realizing that's where I had seen her. That was where she had rested, casually watching TV while I was out on the fire-escape. Taking out the cell, I took a picture of the couch and turned slowly toward the table, thinking of the dinners she had there. I wondered which seat she usually sat in and what type of meals she served. Was she a vegetarian? A vegan? Maybe she was able to prepare gourmet meals? I took a moment and sat in each chair, just to see if I was able to make some kind of connection and to know that at the very least, I had sat in the same place she had. When I looked back at the couch, I stared at the spot where her foot had been and the next thing I knew, I had knelt by the armrest and gently caressed the area. Finally, I moved over and sat down on the couch. As I looked around the room, I took a deep breath and closed my eyes, trying to bring myself back to when I had seen her the first time. I never would have thought back then that I would find myself at her apartment later. The first thing I saw when I opened my eyes was the front door. It was on the left next to the TV. I imagined what it would be like to open that door and find her laying on the couch, watching TV, waiting for me to come home; our home.

Her kitchen was immaculate, which didn't surprise me. The refrigerator was stocked with vegetables, some cold cuts, condiments, juices and a filtered water pitcher. Thinking that she wouldn't mind, I took a glass from the cabinet and poured myself some water. If she was willing to give a stranger some food, I doubted that she would mind a thirsty man drinking some water. Of course at that point I realized that I was drinking from a glass that she probably used. My lips were touching the same spot that hers had touched. Smiling, I thought to myself, "*That would make this our first kiss.*"

After I rinsed out the glass and dried it with a paper towel, I put it back in the cupboard and went to her bedroom. Before I went in, I stood in the doorway and took a moment to look over the space and then I took a picture. The bed was soft and neatly made, almost as if she hadn't slept there. On the far wall she had three framed dried roses – red, white, and yellow. Her pillows carried the scent of her perfume and as I breathed it in, I almost became dizzy with the image of her. It almost seemed as if she were there with me at that moment, smiling and saying my name. "Elsa," I answered before opening my eyes. Her dresser was only slightly messy, a few articles of clothing bunched up in some over-stuffed drawers. In one of them, I found a small white notebook labeled "*Memories*" and I knew that it had to be her journal. I hesitated at first before I opened it, but I couldn't help myself and began to read the thoughts of a teenage Elsa. "October 3, 1999. It's been a month now since I officially began senior year and I can't wait for graduation. Don't get me wrong, these past few years have been great and I love my friends, but honestly if I had to do another year in this place I think I'd die. Demetra says that she wants to go to NYU! I told her that's where I want to go, so we started talking about how great it would be if we went together. Guess we'll see."

I looked around the room and saw a small bookcase next to the desk. Sure enough, I found her high school yearbook on the top shelf between an old dictionary and a bible. I took it down and saw that she went to St. Mary's Prep in Astoria, which meant that she had grown up here. All those years we were so close and yet we had never run into each other. It didn't take me long to find her picture. She really hadn't changed much from when she was in school. Same blonde hair, same kind smile. Elsa Graham, Class President, Valedictorian. Of course she was.

After I read some of the typical, "K.I.T. girl" and "See you at NYU," I went back to her diary. "December 8, 1999. Finally finished the project for Global Studies. I hope Mr. Weinberg likes it, because you know how hard I worked on it. Vanessa said that if I didn't like the grade, I could try to convince him to give me some 'extra credit.' She's so bad! I saw her sit on his desk once with her skirt just barely at her thighs with a cherry blow-pop in her mouth. I told her she was going to get herself in trouble one day, but she laughed and said she just liked teasing. I don't think I could ever do that." I thought about how she ignored all those men who looked at her on the train, and I was sure she got the same kind of attention at work. She knew the kind of impression she left on men but never took advantage of that.

"March 15, 2000. It finally happened! After six months of waiting, it finally happened. He had been trying for a while, but I always said that I wasn't ready. If he only knew that I really wanted to, I just didn't want to give it up that easy. I know the first time is supposed to be 'special' and all that, but I kind of just wanted to get it over with. All my friends have already done it and Vanessa told me what it would be like. She said it would hurt the first time and she was totally right! She said that it would feel better eventually, but that you have to keep doing it for that to happen. I have to admit, I felt a little self-conscious at first, but then I kind of got into it. He was…okay, I guess. Honestly, it was almost over before it began! Ha ha! We're supposed to go out alone this Saturday and he said that his parents would be visiting relatives in Long Island, so I think we might do it again then. I can't believe it!" She ended the entry with a smiley face.

For some reason, I felt myself getting hot after I read that. Of course I didn't think she was a virgin, but then again, I hadn't really thought about that at all. I guess seeing her write about her first time brought it into focus that she wasn't totally...*pure.* I wondered who it was that she was referring to and why she hadn't named him in her diary. Maybe it was just in case someone found it, they wouldn't know all the details, but then why even write about it? Then again, she was 17 when she wrote that. I wondered if she had done it again that Saturday and whatever happened to the guy?

"May 4, 2000. I'm kind of a mess right now. Remember how I said Tartufo has been sick? Well, he died last night. My dad said that keeping him alive was cruel because he was really old, had a bunch of tumors, could barely walk and wasn't going to get any better. Mom, dad, Eddie and I drove him to the vet's office and we each said our goodbyes. God, it was the hardest thing I've ever had to do! I've had Tar since I was a little girl and now all of a sudden, he's gone. It's not fair! I cried the whole night and I could barely concentrate on anything at all today. The girls came by to try and cheer me up earlier. It was really sweet of them and it worked for a while, but now I'm alone again and I can't help feeling sad. I miss my Tar! I'm going to miss practically getting tackled by him as soon as I walk through the door. I'm going to miss the times he would come into my room and lick my face to wake me up. I know I used to complain about taking him for a walk when it was raining but it wasn't so bad. I'd walk him in the rain every day if it meant I could have him back. My poor sweet boy. My Tar!"

On her desk, next to a picture of her with two older people I assumed were her parents, I found a picture of the dog she wrote about and for the first time in years I felt tears in my eyes. I sat down and held the picture in my hands, feeling the tears begin to stream down my cheeks. She wrote that she felt alone back then. I knew exactly what she felt. If she was a senior when that happened, then she had to have been about 17 years old in 2000, which would have made me 14 at the time. Back then, I was still living with my mom's cousin in Jersey. It was my freshman year of high school and it was also my most difficult year. My mom's cousin and his wife had to move because of his job again and so the few kids I had met when I moved in with them went to a different high school than I did, which meant I had to start all over again. Alone was definitely a feeling I was in touch with.

I took a couple of more pictures and noticed that her closet door was slightly ajar. Opening it, I scanned over the blouses, skirts and suits she had neatly hung up. On the bottom she had a four-shelf shoe rack filled with different heels, flats, sneakers and even a pair of boots. The red heels stood out among the rest of course, and I couldn't help but picture her in them again as I held one in my hand. I took one more look before I took a picture and then leaned into the closet. My face was inches away from her clothes and I could smell the lingering aroma that was a combination of perfume and vanilla-brown sugar lotion. After I took another deep breath, I made sure to leave the door in the same position that she had left it.

She had a few bottles of perfume and skin creams on her desk. There were a mix of names and a large bottle of L'Air du Temps in the middle right next to her hairbrush. When I opened the drawer I found some make-up, a couple of different color lipsticks, eyeliner and two small sample bottles of L'Air du Temps. I put one of the small bottles in my pocket. I know it was technically stealing, but I just wanted something to remember her by and I couldn't very well take her diary, so I thought I'd take something she probably wouldn't miss very much. The clock on her nightstand read that it was just past noon, which meant that I had been there for almost 5 hours! People have talked about "losing time" before, but I had never thought it would ever happen to me. I always thought that only people who were kind of crazy went through something like that, not normal every day people.

Obviously, I couldn't just walk out through the front door, so after I checked the alley, I gently closed the window and made my way down the fire escape. Another quick check of the area and I went over the wall and made my way to the street. A little old woman in black was tending to her garden at the house next to where I walked out from, but she barely gave me a glance. Just to be on the safe side, I pulled my hood down over my eyes even more and kept walking toward the avenue. The whole time, I kept feeling the bottle of her perfume in my pocket which made me smile.

The following day, I called out sick again. After seeing her apartment, I got a glimpse into what her life was like in the past but I had no real idea as to what she was like in the present. For that to happen, I needed to see her going about her day. I wanted to see her living life. Watching her on the train or from a window just wasn't enough. I needed more.

The taxi dropped me off about a block away from her building at exactly 6:30 the next morning. I figured she left work at the same time each day, so I waited close by until I saw her leave. As I thought, she left at 7 and looked even more stunning than she had yesterday. As I walked toward her, I wondered if she had drank from the same glass that I had yesterday and realized that I had been smiling at the thought. When I got to the corner, however, I saw Steve walking just ahead of us. I had been so preoccupied with Elsa that it hadn't occurred to me that Steve could also have the same kind of schedule as yesterday. Luckily, he was on his cell again and hadn't seemed to notice anyone else around him.

Up on the platform, he stood relatively close to Elsa. It really started to aggravate me. Other people had crowded in more when they saw the N coming toward the station. I stood a few feet away when the train pulled in. Steve finally put his cell phone away and waited for the doors to open. While everyone else stood right in front of the doors, Elsa stood off to the side to give anyone who wanted to get off the chance to get by. I reached for the cell and realized that it would have been too obvious if I had snapped a picture of her just then. The doors opened and everyone rushed to get inside. Elsa only went in after she saw that there no one else was trying to get out. As I inched forward, the people ahead of me were having trouble getting in. There was someone trying to load two large vertical trunks on wheels into the car and he was having trouble fitting them in between the other passengers. Elsa and Steve were already inside and there were still more people trying to get in after them. I realized that there was a possibility that I could miss the train.

I looked up and down the platform while the idiot ahead of me struggled with the trunks. People sighed and looked for other ways to get on, like I was. The next car over seemed to be clearing up and I knew that doors would soon close. I jogged down to the next car and walked on. Seconds later, the doors tried to close but of course they couldn't because of the guy with the trunks. The other passengers looked at the ceiling in frustration and I tried to find a glimpse of Elsa through the window in the door that led to the next car.

There were too many people in the way, so I just figured that I would bide my time and be patient. At least I knew where she was getting off. I wound up standing next to this guy with a lamp. Not the kind that you put on a table, the other kind. The tall, skinny black poles with the glass cover pointing up. He was almost as tall and thin as the lamp and had one of those old-fashioned, black handlebar moustaches. He had on a light gray three-piece suit and was holding on to the overhead handgrip with one hand and the lamp with the other. When you looked at him, you could almost expect Charlie Chaplin to walk on and tumble into the guy. At one point, the train started to move and this other guy in a suit bumped into him. He apologized, but the lamp guy just kept staring straight ahead. It didn't look like he was staring *at* anything, he wasn't even looking out the window, just looking over everyone's head.

I kept trying to catch a glimpse of her through the window into the next car, but there were too many people in the way. It was the morning rush hour, so more and more people kept shoving their way in at every stop. For a quick second I saw Steve, but then someone stepped in and blocked him. I relaxed. The last thing I wanted was to run into him and have a conversation.

An hour really makes a big difference on the subway. When I would take the train, there weren't as many people. It was still crowded, but there wasn't as much shoving. By the time we got to Queensboro Plaza, I was pushed right up against the guy with the lamp as most of the folks on the car tried to fight their way through to get out. They met head on with everyone on the platform trying to get in. I apologized to the guy, but he didn't seem to notice. He just stood in the same exact position and had the same droopy expression as when I got on. It was almost hard to tell which one was the lamp.

Most of the car cleared when we stopped at Lexington Avenue. People in her car were getting off as well and as I made my way toward the door, I bumped into the lamp. It only tilted a couple of inches and the guy straightened it out right away, but it was the only time I saw him move. He looked right at me, didn't say anything, just…looked. I think I kind of fumbled an "I'm sorry" and was swept out the door by the rest of the crowd. Outside, I saw Elsa and Steve walking toward the staircase. I began to follow them and looked inside the car again. The guy was still looking at me when the train pulled away.

There weren't that many people ahead of me as we walked up the stairs. I still couldn't believe the fucking luck I had with Steve being there at that exact time. We were just as crowded walking up the stairs as we had been in the subway car. The cell was pressing against my thigh now as I tried not to get close to the idiot next to me carrying a briefcase.

For a second she slipped away from me in the crowd when we got to the station from the platform, but I then I saw her going toward the steps leading to the street. People were walking away in all sorts of different directions since the station had more than one way to get to the street above. She was heading towards the 3rd Avenue exit. As we got closer to the stairs, I reached in my pocket and pulled out the cell. She stopped suddenly, as if on cue. I froze. I couldn't let her see me if she decided to turn around, but for some reason I couldn't move. My legs stiffened up and I felt my heart pound against my chest. I could hear the blood rushing in my ears, like a floodgate had been opened. She just stopped. I saw her reach for something inside her jacket, a cell phone. She was making a call.

My legs felt rubbery, but I steadied myself enough to raise my cell and watch her press some buttons. I was hoping for a better shot, something clearer. She wouldn't turn her head, though. She kept looking at the phone. Either she had no reception or she couldn't find the number she wanted. Some kids walked in the line of the shot, talking loudly with each other while they adjusted their schoolbags. I lowered the cell slightly until they got out of the way.

She put the phone to her ear and turned profile for a second. That was all I needed. Aim, click.

As I followed her toward the exit, I heard someone call my name. Steve had stopped at the newsstand and saw me. "I thought that was you, man. How are you?" he smiled, a vertically folded copy of the New York Times tucked under his arm.

"Good, thanks."

"What are you doing around here? Sightseeing?" he smirked. He looked sharp in the navy-blue checkered suit and yellow power tie. A flood of panicked thoughts raced through my mind. *Why would he have asked if I was "sightseeing"? Had he seen me snap the picture? Where was Elsa?*

"Uh…no I…I have a…a meeting, here." I saw her reach the stairs.

"A meeting?"

"Ye…yeah, a meeting. A customer service meeting. Listen Steve, I'm running kind of late, so-"

"Oh, sure man. Listen," he held out his hand and I shook it without looking at him, "let's get together for drinks later if you want. I mean, seeing as how you're going to be in this area."

"Uh…yeah sure. I'll uh, I'll see. I'll give you a call." She was halfway up the steps.

"Great. You have my card, right?"

"Yeah. Listen, I gotta go."

"Ok. See you."

I could've killed him. Really. I could've broken his goddamn neck, if you want to know the truth. He could've ruined everything. She had just reached the top of the steps and was about to disappear when I ran up, taking two at a time. I stopped when I saw her at the corner. She was still talking on the phone, but you couldn't really tell from my angle because she was holding the cell to the other side of her head. Aim, click. Perfect shot. I got her in mid smile. Can you imagine if I had missed that? Fucking Steve!

I held back a little while she crossed the street. The good thing about a place like Manhattan is that you can blend into the crowd at almost any time. Even if she had turned around, she wouldn't have noticed me watching her. Christ, she hadn't even recognized me when I stood right in front of her! I didn't want to think about that just then, though.

I took a quick look around and didn't see Steve anywhere. He probably walked out one of the other exits. It didn't look like anyone had noticed me taking her picture. Of course they hadn't. This was Manhattan. People were walking around with cameras and cell phones taking pictures all the time. Elsa had finished talking on the phone and was heading inside a big, black building along with a crowd of other suits. The entrance took up the block, from corner to corner. There were eight thick steps and then a small patio-like setting before reaching the glass window-front. I guessed that's where she worked.

A huge pair of glass doors next to a revolving door led into the lobby. It was beautiful, almost serene. The walls and floors were sand-colored marble and a long, black security desk stretched across the front. On either side were two steps that brought people past them and to the four rows of elevators behind. Elsa flashed some sort of i.d. badge to the guard standing at the foot of the steps on the left, his counterpart doing the same job on the right. Everyone else was doing the same, so I turned around and walked out through the revolving doors.

At around noon, there were more people going in and out of the place. I had been there the whole morning. She came out at about a quarter after with a group of eight people. They laughed and talked and I saw that I didn't even have to go through the trouble of hiding behind a hot dog vendor on the corner. They walked on by without giving me a second look.

They went to a place called Lee's down the block from the building. It was a Chinese restaurant with favorable newspaper clippings posted on the window by the door as well as a very prominent blue "A" rating, giving you more reasons to stop in for food. I bought a hot dog and watched her from across the street. She and the group sat around the table and once they were settled, she took off her sunglasses.

Everything around me seemed to stop. I had even stopped chewing. Obviously, I was too far away to see the color of her eyes, but it was still the first time that I had ever seen her without the glasses. Slowly, I took the phone out and zoomed in as much as I could. I got pretty close, but I still couldn't make out the color. I took a picture anyway. The waiter came and she read over the menu. Everybody else was still talking. She was beyond words, you know? Every gesture, no matter how simple, was so smooth and fluid. She was graceful and gentle. Even in the way she took a sip of water or the way she smiled at one of them when they spoke to her.

I thought about going in there for a better look. She wouldn't recognize me, that much I knew. Besides, she was so wrapped up with her coworkers that she probably wouldn't take notice of me if I went in there. I could pretend I was going to get take out and if she recognized me, I would tell her what I told Steve earlier.

"Hello, welcome to Lee's. How many in your party?" the well-dressed young lady standing at the podium asked.

"Uh…none. I mean, I'm…alo…uh, not with anyone. Um-" She smiled and waited for me to say something half-way intelligent. I looked around the restaurant and casually glanced over at the table where Elsa and the others were still talking and laughing. By now, the waiter was going around to each of them and writing down their orders. "Table for one, then?"

"Uh, no. No, I'm not, ah, staying." I started to fidget. "Could I just look at a…menu?"

"Sure," she handed me one out of thin air.

"Uh, I'd like to place an order to go if that's alright?"

"Sure. Take as much time as you need."

Sitting down at the bar, I had a clear view of the table. She was practically in front of me. I wasn't quite close enough to follow the conversation, but I caught a few things here and there. *"Can't believe she wore the same thing today," "Swear they're on drugs," "Misplaced the brief," "Left the judge waiting for two days."* Elsa wasn't saying anything, though. She just sat and listened, occasionally, she smiled. There was no way I could get away with taking a picture at the time, so I tried not to stare too much.

"Ready to order?" the waiter surprised me because I jumped slightly when I heard him. "Sorry, sir."

"That's ok. I'm fine. Uh, yeah, I'm ready. Let me have a pint of Moo Goo Gai Pan."

"Anything else?"

"A Coke?"

"Pepsi okay?"

"Fine."

"Moo Goo Gai Pan to go," he repeated and disappeared into the kitchen. I tried to entertain myself by reading the Chinese Zodiac calendar up on the wall, but that didn't last long. The laughter from the table soon cut in and I found myself staring at her again, until she dropped her napkin.

She hadn't realized that it was on the floor. If I picked it up, she would definitely see me. That would make following her that much harder; never mind taking her picture again. Then again, I thought that it could open the door for something else. I stood up from the bar and took a step toward her. Nobody noticed. Another step, she took another sip of water and listened to something that some jerk-off across the table was saying. The napkin was resting on the floor, bunched up and waiting. She still hadn't noticed it and still hadn't noticed me. I took another step. Two more and I would be right there. Her left leg moved slightly and I was able to see her ankle. It was right above the strap of the light gray shoes that matched her suit. She was wearing nude pantyhose. Either that or stockings. No, it was pantyhose. It had to be pantyhose.

I tried to think of something clever to say. In another step, I would bend down and pick up the napkin. Maybe even…brush against her ankle. What could I say? What would be something clever? Something she probably hadn't heard a million times before from a million other men trying to get her attention? *"Seems you're always dropping something."* That would be a way to remind her about the time I returned the dry cleaning ticket to her. "Nah, too hokey," I thought – or did I say that out loud? *"Excuse me Ms? I think you dropped this."* Simple, straight, to the point. Maybe she would appreciate the directness. No clever little lines, just a simple kindness. Yeah, that would work. Someone at the table sitting on the other side looked at me. I was about to bend down to pick up the napkin, one more step would've done it, when the waiter rushed over and grabbed it. He handed it back to her and she quietly thanked him. When he turned to me, he asked if I was waiting for an order. A couple of the folks at the table looked over at me, including Elsa.

Blue. They were blue.

Chapter Fifteen

The following day at work, I think I asked people to repeat what they had said at least twice in every conversation, both on and off the phone. At one point, I was five minutes into a call before realizing that the customer was speaking to me in Spanish. I transferred it to Sofia since she handled all of our Hispanic customers. Brian and George kept asking me if I was okay and I told both of them that I was fine, just a little tired.

I didn't see her on the way home. It would've been nice, but it was okay because I was still on kind of a high from when I saw her at the restaurant. She had looked right at me. Shit, she looked through me and into my soul. I never saw eyes that color before. I thought you had to die to see something like that. The rest of the table was looking at me too, but I couldn't describe a single one of them. As stupid as it sounds, I actually felt naked as I stood there. The waiter was hoping for an answer and I'm sure everybody else was wondering who the hell I was and what I was doing. But I couldn't stop looking at her. It's like her eyes were holding me up in mid-air.

"Sir? Are you waiting for an order? Moo Goo Gai Pan?"

Somebody dropped a glass somewhere behind me and I snapped out of it. "Yeah."

"It's ready," he rushed past me to see about the glass.

"Hi," I said, still looking at her. She smiled and nodded. "I...I was just going to pick up your –"

"You look familiar. Do I know you from somewhere?" she asked.

"Uh...I don't think so. Maybe. You ah...you look kind of familiar to me, too." She smiled at me and I think I smiled back.

"My...order's ready. Have a good day," I said. She half-nodded and turned her attention back to her table. I paid for my food and left.

I didn't want to risk her seeing me again, so I went home after that. Throughout the whole ride back, I thought about her. Then I thought about Steve. I wondered if he had seen me take that picture of her at the station. What would he think about that? What if he didn't buy that story I fed him about having a meeting? Would he say something to her if he ever bumped into her on the train? They lived pretty close to each other so it was possible for them to have met. He would probably think that I was some sort of a weirdo. I decided that I had to find out if he suspected anything.

I waited until about 6:30 that night and then called him from my cell. No answer and I sort of fumbled over what to say on the answering machine, but eventually, I told him it was me. His wife picked up after that. "Everest? Hi, it's Melissa."

"Oh, hi Melissa. How are you?"

"Okay, thanks. How's it going with you?"

"Fine. Listen, is Steve there?"

"No, he's not home yet. He called and said he would be working late. Do you want me to tell him you called?"

"Uh…yeah. Yeah, please."

"Okay. Does he have your number?"

"No. But uh…actually, I'm having a little…trouble with my phone, so he wouldn't be able to reach me anyway. Tell him I'll call him tomorrow."

"Okay."

"Thanks, Melissa."

"Nice talking with you, Everest." I hung up and decided to try and reach him at his office but he wasn't picking up there either.

I uploaded the pictures I took of Elsa and after I stared at them for a while, I decided to turn in early. Steve wouldn't have suspected anything. There wasn't any reason for him to suspect anything. I mean, even if he had seen me take a picture, what would be the big deal? Nothing, right? Besides, there would be no way for him to know that I had taken a picture of Elsa.

I called Steve the next day right after lunch and he picked up.

"Buddy! Hey, I got your message last night. How are you?"

"Good thanks. How are you?"

"Not too bad. Pile of papers on my desk, but you know how it is."

"Yeah."

"So what's up?"

"Oh, uh…I just wanted to see if that…drink offer still stands. Thought we could meet up after work."

"Ah. Um, what time are you thinking?"

"Whatever. I get out of work at 5."

"Ooo, um, can't do that today. How about Friday? Friday okay with you?"

"Sure. Friday's fine."

"Ok. Why doncha come by at around 7?" After he gave me his address, I told him I would see him then.

I didn't know what to bring, so I showed up at the door at around ten after seven holding a six-pack of Corona. Steve let me in with a big smile and a pat on the back. "Melissa is in the kitchen," he said and showed me into the living room. "Have a seat and I'll be right back." He took the beer in with him to the kitchen. Steve and Melissa lived in a two-bedroom apartment on the second floor of a two family house, just a few blocks away from Elsa. The living room looked like something out of an Ikea catalog and the whole place smelled like air freshener. In the center of the room they had a burgundy area rug, accented with small flowers and a mahogany coffee table with a glass top. I sat on the slipcovered, burgundy sofa against the wall and looked at the silver-framed wedding picture on top of the 55" flat screen. It was a good contrast to the eggshell white walls. The polished hardwood floor was still shiny and for a second I felt like I should've wiped my feet before I walked on it.

"Fuck it," I thought.

Melissa walked in and I accidentally stubbed her toe when I stood up and moved to greet her. "Sorry," I said.

"It's…okay. Don't worry about it. How are you?" she winced.

"Okay, thanks. How are you? Beside the toe, I mean."

"Fine, thanks. I'm so glad that you could come."

"It was nice of you two to invite me."

"It's not very often that we get to do this. Steve's always working and I barely have time to do anything by the time I get out of work myself. This is a welcome change."

"Thanks."

"Can I get you something to drink?"

"Sure."

"What would you like?"

"What do you have?"

"Uh…lots," she laughed. She opened the door to a smaller room by the TV. They had one of those mini-bars that you could roll around.

Black, of course, with two compartments in the front that opened to reveal all the booze they had. "Screwdriver?" I asked.

Steve came back in while she was fixing my drink and sat down on the recliner next to the sofa. "So, Everest. How's it going?"

"Okay, I guess, Steve. How about with you?"

"More or less the same. Work okay?"

"It's work."

"I know what you mean. I had this real asshole client earlier today. He just took over as President for Renaissance Airways."

"Oh, that new airline company."

"Well, they're not all that new, been out there for a couple of years. Anyway, he's a real hardass. Wants to totally change the company's image and he's hounding me day and night about the account."

"Sounds rough," I said as Melissa handed me my drink.

"Still, nobody said this was going to be easy. I'd much rather be behind my desk all day, though, than one of those poor schmucks stuck in a cube for eight hours, know what I mean?"

"Yeah, I do."

Melissa disappeared into the kitchen again and Steve and I were finally left alone. I wasn't quite sure how to broach the subject, though. How could I bring it up without it being weird? "So, what a coincidence bumping into you the other day at the station," I said.

"Yeah, how about that? I had never seen you on the train in the mornings. Is that what time you usually head into the city or was it just for the meeting?"

"Uh, it was just for the meeting."

"What was it on?"

"Huh?"

"The meeting? What was it for?"

"Oh, it was just some…stupid…customer service meeting thing. You know, how to talk to customers, remain calm. All that crap."

"Sounds riveting."

"So how about you? You always take the train at that hour?"

"Uh yeah, pretty much. You know, sometimes a little earlier if I've got a lot of work to do."

"Must get pretty boring seeing the same faces over and over again, huh?"

"Not really. To be honest, I don't even notice the other people. Until they're standing on my feet," he laughed.

Melissa joined us and said that dinner would be ready soon. We talked about what we were like in high school again and Steve brought out the old yearbook. Melissa shrieked and giggled when we flipped it open to his picture and then again when we looked at mine. In the back, we found where I had signed. "Steve, Thanks for being such a great friend. Good luck, Everest."

Melissa had made spinach lasagna with garlic bread and brought out a bottle of some homemade red wine. We sat around a large oak table in the dining room between the kitchen and living room. "My father made this," she said, filling our glasses.

"He makes his own wine?"

"Ever since he was a kid. My grandfather use to do it and his father used to do it."

"Family tradition," Steve said, raising a glass. We toasted and began to eat. She was a good cook, I must admit. Everything seemed so right with the two of them. Nice little apartment, nice food, nice wine.

Steve's cell went off at one point. He had it on vibrate and he excused himself to answer take it in the kitchen. "So Everest, are you seeing anyone? Dating anyone?" Melissa asked.

"No, not dating anyone."

"Interested in anyone?"

"What?"

"Are you interested in anyone? Do you like somebody?"

"Um...I...don't know. I really don't have time for that sort of thing. Work keeps me really busy and by the time I get home, I'm so tired I don't have the energy to do anything."

"I know what you mean. You wouldn't think that staring into a computer monitor or reading sales figures all day would wear you out, but it takes its toll on you after a while."

"Yeah, it does."

"Steve gets home so late sometimes, I wonder why he doesn't just put a cot in his office."

He came back in and apologized for taking so long. "Who was it?" she asked.

"Carl. He wanted to know if I had gone over the sales figures for the PharmEx account. He thinks there may be a problem."

"Really?"

"Yeah, which means that I'm probably going to have to go in tomorrow for a couple of hours."

"What about our tickets to see *Phantom* tomorrow in the afternoon?"

"I know sweetie, but what am I supposed to do?"

"Tell Carl that you have plans that can't be broken."

"Melissa, I've been working on this account for the past three weeks and we're almost done. I can't bail out now when we're so close."

"What about the tickets?"

"Well…why don't you ask your mom? She loves all that Broadway stuff."

"I guess. Let me call her now and see if she can make it. Excuse me." She dropped her napkin on her chair and left the room. Steve looked at me and shrugged. "Married life," he sighed and poured the rest of the wine in both our glasses.

After Melissa's mom told her that she would go with her on Saturday, she cleared off the table and Steve and I went outside for a smoke. Well, he smoked, I just hung around. He offered me a cigarette but I didn't want one. I hadn't smoked in five years.

"Quit, huh?"

"Yeah."

"Yah, I gotta do that too. I'm up to a pack a day."

"Wow."

"You're not kidding. Expensive."

"I can imagine."

I was feeling a little buzz from the wine as we went upstairs and I told him that I was going to go home. "You sure, man? It's early."

"Yeah, I know. I just have to uh, get up...get up early tomorrow."

"Oh, okay. Melissa, Everest is going." She came out of the kitchen, wiping her hands on a red and white-checkered dishtowel. "You're leaving already?" she smiled.

"Yeah, I got an early day tomorrow so I'm gonna take off."

"Well, thanks for coming by," she leaned in and kissed me on the cheek. Her perfume stayed in the air around me for a while.

"No, thanks for having me. Dinner was great."

"You want to call a cab?" he asked.

"No thanks. I'm gonna…stop by a store and uh, pick up the paper."

"Okay. Honey, I'm just gonna walk him out," he said, turning to
Melissa and giving her a quick kiss.

We stood in front of the house and he lit up another cigarette.

"Thanks again for having me over," I said.

"Nice time," he smirked, blowing smoke in the air and shaking my
hand.

"Yeah it was. You got a great wife and a nice place. I'm…glad
everything turned out good for you." He cocked an eyebrow and
took another drag. Looking down at the sidewalk, he kicked away a
small rock. "Thanks," he said. It almost looked like he had said it to
the rock. "So what about you? You doing okay?"

"Me? Yeah, I'm fine," I answered. He reached in his pocket, pulled
out his cell phone that was vibrating and took a couple of steps
away. Once he checked the number he asked me to excuse him and
answered the call. "Hi, hang on a sec?" He came back to me and
shook my hand again. "Listen, I gotta take this. Office stuff."

"Sure, no problem."

"I had a great time."

"Me too. Thanks for dinner."

"You're welcome, anytime. Call me and we'll do this again. Maybe we'll meet up in the city."

"Sounds good." He held the phone back up to his ear and walked to the front of the next house.

Chapter Sixteen

As I sat in Hoyt Park and stared at her building, I thought about Melissa and Steve. Melissa and Steve. I really meant what I had said to him. Things had gone really well for him and I was happy for him. Truth be told, I was envious. It looked like he had a job that he didn't hate having to go to in the morning and Melissa seemed to make home just that, home. It was someplace warm and nice and safe from all the bullshit going on in the world. I wondered then if I would ever have that...with Elsa.

At about a quarter after 11, I snuck around back and looked at her bedroom window. It was still dark, but the living room light was on. She was home. Home on another Friday. I felt the cell in my pocket again and climbed up the fire escape. The TV was on, but I wasn't able to see her that time. I saw some movement inside and a minute or so later, she walked out of the living room as she spoke on her cell and headed in my direction.

I stood up against the wall near the window, afraid to move. If she were to have caught me there it would really have been the end of it. There would have been no way to explain that. Whenever I

saw her shadow come through the window, it felt like I couldn't

breathe. She was so close, just on the other side of the wall. As

stupid as it may have been, I felt I had to risk it. Crouching as low

as I could, I slowly crept toward the window and took another glance

to make sure no one had been watching me from the houses across

the way. The windows on the floors below me were still dark and

the houses across the way seemed to be busy doing their own thing

to notice me. Besides, I had deliberately worn dark clothes for that

reason. Black jeans, dark purple shirt, dark gray hoodie. I had

considered bringing along a mask, but I thought that that would have

been too weird. As I got to the edge of the window, I eased the cell

out of my pocket and carefully peeked around the edge.

She stood in front of her closet with her back facing me, no

longer on her cell. A silky, white bathrobe covered her, tied securely

at the waist. Her hair was loose and she ran her fingers through it

and messed it up some. She slid some hangers around back and

forth, apparently looking for something appropriate. Whoever she

had spoken with had obviously proposed something good for her to want to get dressed at that hour. With her hands on her hips, she stepped back and looked at her clothes. I quickly aimed and snapped a shot, not realizing that I had left the flash on.

I pressed myself up against the wall again. How could I have been so stupid?! She had to have seen that flash and there wasn't any lighting that it could have been chalked up to. Her shadow grew bigger as she approached the window and I realized she was going to check out where the flash had come from. The stairs leading back down were right in front of me, but if I had moved even the slightest inch, she would definitely have seen me. Her shadow stayed there and I saw it move from side to side, up and down. For a second, I thought about going over the fire escape and trying to climb down from the side. I had actually started to pray.

Eventually, she left the window and I waited a few minutes for me to calm down, before I inched towards the stairs. I figured since I had lucked out by not getting caught, I had better not tempt Fate or God or whoever. One picture, that's all I had. And I had almost gotten caught taking it. The light in her room went out and I thought

I'd take one last look before I left. No camera or anything, just me.
I poked around the edge of the window and saw her as she walked
down the hall toward the living room, still in her bathrobe. The soft
white bottom of her feet flashing me as she walked further away.

She wasn't anywhere to be seen, anyway and while it was hard
for me to tear myself away, I managed to get back down to the alley
without being spotted by anyone. The light came on again and I hid
behind the trash. She didn't go to the window that time, though.
After a few minutes, she turned it off and I saw the bathroom light
flick on. She was probably getting ready to go out. Of course she
was. Why would somebody like her be home on another Friday? I
thought about going over the wall behind me and leaving through the
driveway, but as I started to climb over, I noticed another light go on
in her apartment.

I made my way toward the front until I got just underneath her
window. The curtains were open and I was able to look right up at
her kitchen. The thought occurred to me that maybe she wasn't
going to go out. Or, maybe she was getting something to drink

before she left. Whatever it was that she was doing, I couldn't see her. Out of the corner of my eye, I saw someone walk past the front of the alley. I immediately crouched back under the windows again, but I didn't think that whoever it was saw me. It looked like they had gone inside her building.

A few minutes later I looked up again and saw that the light was still on. I was itching to go back up that fire escape again, but I didn't want to risk it. Once was enough. Ok, maybe not enough, but it was going to have to do. At that moment, I saw a pair of hands draw the curtains and lower the shades. They weren't hers though.

Whoever had gone into the building while I was in the alley was obviously going to see her. A man. Some guy was visiting her. Some guy who needed to draw the shades in the kitchen. A slew of questions ran through my head. Why would he need to draw the shades in the kitchen? What was he doing? What was he doing to her? Who the hell was he?

I went back to the trash bins. Her bedroom was still dark. When I peered down the alley, I saw that the kitchen had gone dark too. There were no lights on in the apartment. Again the questions popped up. Had he taken her out? Was he a friend or family member? I thought that if I snuck out to the front I could catch a glimpse of them from Hoyt Park as they came out. As I tried to think of ways to figure out what was going on, I noticed that the shades in her bedroom had been drawn.

I sat in Hoyt Park for an hour before I realized that either I had missed them or…they were still in her apartment; with the shades drawn. The phone suddenly felt heavier in my pocket and I paced around for another half hour or so. After that, I wandered around for a while. Dazed, I eventually wound up walking down 21st Street toward Ravenswood.

The Q19A stopped right in front of me as I sat on a bench at the bus stop. "You getting' on?" the driver called out. I shook my head, the doors shut and he took off. I was about a mile away from my apartment, but I was tired from all the walking so I had sat down.

Salsa music blared from the bar behind me whenever anyone opened

the door. Spanish was shouted from one person to another and I

recognized a few of the words. "Cabrón!"

"Hijo de puta!"

"Maricón!" I stood up to start walking when suddenly a fight

erupted in the bar and spilled outside close to me. One of the

customers bumped into me as he tried to get a better view. Some

bald guy with a goatee was really pounding on this other guy with

black, greasy hair. They were both dressed completely in black and

the only difference was the placement of the hair. One on his head,

the other on his chin. The guy with the greasy hair had managed to

get Mr. Clean in a headlock. It didn't last long, though. Mr. Clean

punched him right in the balls and the guy let him go pretty quickly.

Red lights started flashing and a cop car came rushing up. When

the cops got out of their car and made their way to the scene where

people had separated the guys in the fight, I started walking down

the block. As I walked back home, I thought about the fight and

how I heard the impact of their fists against each other. Over and

again until blood was drawn. I know how this is going to sound but…it felt good to watch. It really almost felt like I was the one fighting. I wasn't rooting for either one in particular, just whoever threw the most punches. It was a good fight. Over too quickly, but it was still good. Street fights don't last long. Not if they're real. It's not like you see in the movies where all these guys keep coming back with their face all busted and blood gushing everywhere. That's bullshit. Here, if you go down, they make sure that you stay down.

My mind kept going back to Elsa. *What the hell was going on in that apartment? Who was that guy?* It was all I could think of. I was on fire while I walked down the avenue. Panhandlers asked me for money, kids on the corner would try to mess with me, but I just kept walking. I couldn't even really hear what they were saying. All I could think about was that guy. Whoever he was. Right now, he was enjoying her in ways that I could only dream about, and *had* dreamt about! Who was he? What did he do for a living? How did he know her? Did he love her? *Really* love her? "Son of a bitch!" I yelled.

Not surprisingly, I ran into Simone. She was done up in her best gear and had just come out of the grocery store. "Hey there!"

"Hi."

"My luck's getting betta awl the time."

"What do you mean?"

"Well, it's the second time I seen you at night. You nevah come out at night. Always up in your 'partment."

"Just coming back from a friend's."

"How's your head?"

"What?"

"Your head? You evah go to the doctah?"

"Oh. Um, no. No, I never went to the doctor. I'm okay. Thanks for asking, though."

We walked to the building together. She was holding a small brown bag. "So watchu doin' tonight? Goin' back to your place?"

"I don't know. Probably."

"Don't sound like much fun."

"What are you doing?" She just looked at me and smiled. I should've known better than to have asked. Friday night was probably her busiest night. "You wanna stop off at my place? Party?" she asked.

Ordinarily, I would have told her "no" right on the spot. But the way I was feeling, I couldn't decide right away. I felt worse than I when I fell off her fire escape. We stood in front of her apartment and she was looking up at me and smiling. I looked her up and down and noticed for the first time how she actually didn't look that bad. Her breasts were pushed up toward me, her mini-skirt was only a half-inch away from her crotch and she had on red high-heels. It reminded me of the kind that Elsa wore on the train that time. *She was getting some, why the hell shouldn't I?* I thought. Hell, she hadn't even remembered me at the grocery store!

Simone had left the TV on in her apartment, so we were greeted by an *I Love Lucy* episode on Nickelodeon when we walked into her dark living room. She locked the door behind me and told me to sit on the couch and make myself comfortable. While she went into the next room, I looked around the mess in her apartment and all ashtrays spilling over with cigarette butts. I turned my attention back to *Lucy*. It was the one where everybody was practicing what to do when it was time for Lucy to give birth. That's a great episode.

She came back and sat down next to me, lighting a cigarette. "You smoke?" she asked, blowing a cloud over us.

"No."

"Mind if I do?"

"Nope." The live studio audience on the TV laughed at something and we both watched for a while. "Wan' somethin' to drink?"

"No thanks. I'm okay. You go ahead though, if you want."

Smiling, she left the room and came back with a small vile of coke. "Hit?" she asked.

"I'm good." She did two lines, rubbed her nose and got up to put the vile away.

When she came back and sat down, she put her hand on my knee and rubbed my leg. "You're pretty trusting," I said.

"What do you mean?"

"Well, the coke, inviting me in here to uh…party."

"You a cop?"

"No."

"I knew that."

"But how do you know that I won't say anything to anyone?"

"Oh you mean and ruin my rep aroun' here?" I laughed at that, she made sense. "First of all, you don' look like the type that tawks too much. Second, like anyfuckingthing you say is gonna make a difference about how these people think of me. Especially that ol' woman, wuh her name?"

"Hilda?"

"Yeah, Hilda. That's right. Remember the other day when she saw us tawkin'? If looks could kill."

"Hilda's okay. She's just…old fashioned."

"She nosy. She always be stickin' her ol' nose in places it don belong. I hate that shit. Me? I min' my bidnes and don mess with nobody here."

"Well, uh…I'm…I'm here." She smiled again and leaned in for a kiss. At the last second, I kind of turned my head and she kissed my neck.

We fooled around on the couch for a while, she was pretty aggressive that one. There was some petting here, a grab there, a stroke here. She kicked off one of her heels and I stopped. "Was the mattah?"

"Uh, nothing."

"Wuhs wrong?"

"Nothing's wrong. Um…could you, uh…could you keep…your uh…"

"You want me to keep my heels awn?"

"Yeah."

"No problem," she smiled. As she leaned over and grabbed her shoe, her hand reached over and grabbed my dick. "You got $60 on you baby?"

"$60?"

"For $60, I'll do everything."

"Uh, yeah. Yeah, hold on." She put her shoe on and I reached in my pocket to get the money, but I couldn't get a good hold on the bills because of the phone. I moved it around, but it kept getting in the way so I pulled it out and put it on the coffee table in front of us.

"Ooo, nice phone."

"Yeah," I said and counted out three twenties.

She folded the money into her purse and took the cell out of my hand before I could put it back in my pocket. "This is a nice one, baby."

"Yeah, it's okay."

"This is a nice one too," she smiled as she rubbed my crotch.

"Thank you," I said. She smiled and hiked up her skirt to show me that she wasn't wearing any panties. The tuft of black, wiry hair between her legs looked messy and it was pretty thick. Simone pulled off her tube top, undid her bra and her breasts bounced out, big, round, with a few stretch marks. She pulled me toward her and I began to kiss her chest, holding her breasts in my hands and massaging them as I started to make my way to one of her nipples.

"Easy baby, don' squeeze 'em so hard," she said. I loosened my hands and flicked her hard, brown nipple with my tongue before taking it in my mouth. She started to grind against me and as I closed my eyes, one of her heels touched the back of my leg. One of her red heels. I started to think about Elsa. "Easy baby, easy," she said. I kissed her gently and began to play with her other nipple.

"Das it. Dat's nice," she sighed. Her hand reached between us and

she began to massage my bulge again. "You ready aintcha?" she

asked and undid my pants. I kneeled on the couch and let her finish,

looking over at her foot in the red shoe.

She held it in her hand and stroked me lightly. "Nice, baby. Real

nice. Yeah." My eyes were closed while she used her hand and I

kept getting flashes of Elsa. Elsa on the train, reading. Elsa at the

grocery. Elsa at the restaurant. "You gonna love this baby, watch."

Simone had stopped and reached for her purse again, pulling out a

condom. She put it on me and kissed my stomach. Next thing I felt

was Simone taking me in her mouth and all I could think about was

Elsa at her window. Her other hand stroked my leg, but I kept my

eyes closed. She drew me in deep and she stopped once to use her

hand before putting it back in her mouth again. Elsa looked great in

that bathrobe. She looked fantastic and I got a picture of it! Simone

stopped, laid on her back on the couch and inched her waist toward

me. I hovered over her and she reached down to guide me inside of

her. My eyes were closed when she wrapped her legs around me and

I felt her heat on my skin. But all I thought about, the fantasy that played out in my mind wasn't that I was with Simone. In my mind, I imagined that I was with Elsa.

"Do it baby," she said. At that point, I opened my eyes and looked at her, looked in her eyes. They were brown, but in my mind, I saw sky blue eyes that stared back at me and begged me to slip inside her. I wanted to do it and forget the whole fucking world and the phone calls and the fire escapes. Every part of me wanted to be with Elsa and I imagined her wanting to be with me as well, a life together. One of her hands grabbed my hip and pulled me closer. No one else understood, how could they until they had seen her. And even then, they wouldn't get it because everyone was so wrapped up in their little fucking worlds that they could never see her for all of the wonderful things that she was. Everyone on the train, the neighborhood, her job, none of them had a clue. She was better than all of them and of course, she was too modest to even know it. "Yeah baby," she moaned underneath me. But I knew it. I knew from the first moment I first saw her. Her hips lifted as she pulled me into her.

Elsa. Every move she made was perfect. It was better than perfect. It was pure. "Mmm, damn baby," she groaned. I think that was the best way I could describe her. She seemed pure, like a child's dream. Sweat dripped off my face as we moved against each other, my eyes closed and focused on Elsa. Even though we didn't know each other, I knew we were meant to be together. "God, yes baby," she whispered. Her hands held the sides of my face and pulled me in for a kiss. Everything felt so good and while it wasn't exactly perfect, it was almost the way I had pictured it with Elsa. At that moment, a sickening thought crept into my mind. *What was she doing with him?* "What?" I heard Simone ask.

What was happening in her apartment? I shook my head at Simone's question and focused on Elsa. What was that about? I thought, if I had stayed on the fire escape, I could've hidden against the wall until I saw his face. Instead, all I had seen was a drawn curtain, a pulled down shade. I had been shut out. I had been shut out because of him. This faceless asshole who didn't care about her, not the way I did. Yeah, they were with each other that night, but was I supposed to stop being a part of her life because he was probably taking advantage of her?! "Don't stop," she said and I realized it made sense. I couldn't stop, not when we were so close, when it was so obvious we were going to be together! That was all that mattered. Yeah, she was the one. She had to be. "Yes baby!" Simone yelled and I felt myself explode inside her. *She better be.*

When I opened my eyes, Simone had a smile on her face that had made me feel sick. I slowly got off of her and took the condom off. "Baby, you gotta come back soon," she said. A wave of nausea swept over me and I steadied myself against the arm of the couch. "Wuhs the matter baby? You okay?" I ignored her and got dressed, she sat up and slid next to me, rubbing my shoulders. "Wuhs wrong?"

"Nothing. I'm fine. I just can't..."

"It looked like you had fun."

"Fun?" I looked at her sharply.

"Uh...yeah. Yeah, we both did. I know I did," she smiled and kissed my cheek. It was as if my mind suddenly cleared and this sense of humiliation and guilt settled in. She had said it was "fun". That's not how I thought about what had happened. Elsa was something

beautiful and pure and I had debased that by fucking Simone.

Simone, of all people who was as different from Elsa as night and

day. How could I have done that?! I rationalized that it had been

because of how hurt I felt over Elsa being with some other guy, but

that didn't mean that what I had done was right. What Simone and I

had done wasn't fun, it was wrong and disgusting. All I wanted to

do was leave.

When I finished getting myself together, I stood up and tried to

undo the locks on her door. "Hold awn," she said and got dressed.

She walked over and held my hand. "You sure you okay?"

"Yeah, I'm fine. I…I'm fine. Thanks." She looked at me, as if she

were trying to figure something out. Finally, she undid the locks and

I slipped out.

When I woke up the next morning, I was balled up in a corner of

the bed with the sheets pulled up to my ears. I hadn't taken off my

clothes so I reeked of cigarettes but I couldn't get up to change. The

previous night's shame still hung over me, and I couldn't help wonder what Elsa was doing at that moment. Had she woken up next to him? Had he spent the night? Were they sleeping or had they gotten up to get breakfast and talk about last night? The phone was still in my pocket and I took it out and looked at the picture of her in front of her closet. I couldn't see her face, but she looked perfect. And I realized that while she might have showed someone else how perfect she was, I was with a whore.

That afternoon, I went out and kind of hurried past Simone's door. Hilda was sitting outside with Cherry, of course, and she gave me a big smile when she saw me. "Well hello! And how are you feeling?"

"Oh fine, thanks. How are you, Hilda?" I asked, ignoring Cherry as she wagged her tail lifted herself on her hind legs.

"Fine, thank you. How's your head?"

"Better, thanks."

"You hear about Mrs. Perez in 5E?"

"No."

"Passed away in the middle of the night. Heart attack."

"Wow."

"She was only 57. Her husband Paul said that she hadn't been feeling well and went to bed early. When he woke up this morning, she was already gone."

"That sounds terrible."

"Oh, he was devastated. Poor man. She was a good woman, too. Hard working, always had a smile on her face for people. She was a nurse over at Mt. Sinai."

"Really?"

"She left that man with two kids all by himself."

"That's a shame."

"Makes you think about things. You never know what's gonna happen tomorrow."

"That's true. Listen Hilda, I gotta go. Sorry to hear about Mrs. Perez."

"Okay, Everest. Do you think you could walk Cherry for me later?"

"Sure. I'll be by at the same time."

I wanted to find out if that son of a bitch had stayed there with her the whole night. By the time I got to the park, the courts were already taken and there were some parents on the playground with their kids. It was too bright for me to sneak around to the back, so I just hung around the park and bought an ice-cream cone at around noon.

At 2:30, I saw her walk out. She was alone and dressed in the same gray sweats that I saw her with that last time. I followed her to the corner, and saw her say hello to some people she recognized from the neighborhood. After that, she went into the grocery store. *Was she buying food?* I wondered. *Food for him, maybe? Something that they could munch on together before he…slept with her again?*

Her eyes were hidden behind the sunglasses, of course. She picked up a hand basket and stepped back outside to look over some fruit. It wasn't until I bumped into her that she looked up at me. "Excuse me," she said.

"Oh, that's okay. It was my fault," I said. She sort of did a double take when I spoke to her. I picked up an orange and carefully looked it over. Out of the corner of my eye, I could see that she was still looking at me. "Slim pickings," I sighed. She moved a bit closer. When I looked at her, even though I couldn't see her eyes, I could tell that she was staring at me and trying to figure out where she knew me from. "I'm sorry, I don't mean to stare but you look very familiar," she smiled. *She smiled.*

"Oh…uh, I get that a lot."

"Do you live in this neighborhood?" Was she actually having a conversation with me?

"Yeah. Well, close by. You?"

"Me too. Close by. Sorry, I know how this may sound but I could swear that I know you from someplace." I smiled at her and shrugged my shoulders. A few seconds later, I saw the look of recognition that came over her face.

I was worried that maybe there was a chance that she had seen me take a picture of her and I hadn't noticed? She took a step forward and I started to sweat. "The um…the restaurant. Oh, what's the name of that place? The Chinese restaurant. Lee's?"

"Oh? Do you go there?" I asked, picking up another orange.

"I was there recently and that's where I saw you. Do you remember? I was at a table with a group of people and had dropped my napkin. You were going to pick it up but then a waiter got it first."

"Mmm, vaguely. Oh, wait a minute. Yeah, yeah I remember.

Wow, good memory," I lied, still a little hurt that she hadn't

remembered having met at the train station.

"Well, thanks for the effort."

"Huh?"

"To pick up my napkin."

"Oh that. That was nothing."

"That's so funny seeing you here now. So you shop here?"

"Not very often. Actually, I haven't even been in this neighborhood

for a while. At least a couple of months."

"I always buy fruit here."

"Well, I like their taste in oranges." *Like their taste in oranges?!*

"What are you getting?"

"Nothing much. Probably some bananas, maybe some apples."

"Sounds good."

I left her outside and pretended to look for some things in the

store. She kept her eyes on the fruit while I peeked over the aisles

and stole a glance now and then. The whole time I tried to think of

something clever to say, something that would grab her attention and would make her want to talk to me. Honestly, I couldn't think of a

fucking thing. Here was this wonderful opportunity to finally talk to

the woman I'd been following for weeks and nothing came to mind.

Not that I was ever very good at that sort of thing, but I would've

taken anything at that point. A simple joke, a clever anecdote or

funny story about an uncle who didn't even exist. Anything.

She went back in the store, walked to the frozen section, and

picked up some yogurt and whipped cream. When I casually walked

over to that area, I helped her pick up a gallon of milk, waiting for

her to make room in the basket so that I could put it in. "Thanks,"

she smiled.

"No problem."

"It seems you're always coming to my rescue." I tried to come up

with something to say. "I'm Everest."

"Nice to meet you. I'm Elsa."

Even if she hadn't remembered my face, you'd think that she'd

remember a name like mine, since you don't really hear it that often.

Still, I was happy that she at least recognized me. We were actually having a conversation! So what that she hadn't remembered me from before! "So you all done?" she asked.

"Um, yeah. I…I think so. You?"

"Yup. Gotta head back home." We walked up to the register and paid for our things. I held the door open for her to get out. "You heading this way too?" she asked as she saw that I was going with her to the corner.

"Oh, uh…yeah. Yeah I'm gonna uh, take a walk over to um, Ditmars. Gotta stop over at the pharmacy."

"Oh," she smiled.

As we walked I saw that she kept looking over across the street. "So um, what do you do, Elsa?"

"I'm a para-legal."

"Really? That's great."

"It's okay. Office is in midtown which is why we went to Lee's that day. Are you by that area?"

"Um, not exactly. I'm more Downtown, but we had a…a meeting, in the city. I mean in Midtown that day."

"Hmm, small world."

"Yeah. So um, you…you been in Astoria long?" I noticed that she hadn't asked what I did for a living. Wouldn't that have been the courteous thing to do?

"Um, yeah pretty much. Well, it was nice meeting you." We had gotten to the corner already and she was going to cross the street.

"Yeah, same here."

"Maybe we'll bump into each other again sometime."

"That would great."

"Take care."

It was tough not to stare at her as she walked away and take a picture, but I couldn't risk it. I had to try and act cool just in case she turned around to check me out or someone in her neighborhood saw me look at her. When I got to the corner and made a left toward Ditmars, I stopped and peered around the corner, but she was long gone by then. After a few minutes, I went over to the driveway from the 24th Avenue entrance, dropped my "groceries" into the first garbage can I saw and walked until I got to where I could see the top of her building from behind the wall. It was too high up to look at her window, so after I checked to make sure there was nobody around, I climbed the wall. I know it was a pretty stupid thing to do considering it was broad daylight outside, but I had to try and get a look at her window. I had to see if the shades were closed.

There were voices, however, when I got to the top stopped me. The porters that worked the building were taking out the trash, but they hadn't seen me. I held my breath, waited for a few minutes until they went back inside the building and I looked at her window. The shades were drawn.

Chapter Seventeen

I didn't sleep the rest of that weekend. Hell, it was tough for me to do anything else but think about her. Even as I walked Cherry around the neighborhood, I thought about her. Everything had changed. Now that we met a second time, it would be that much harder to follow her, but I thought that maybe that was a good thing. It meant that if I saw her on the train, I could go up to her and say hello. I wouldn't really have needed to follow her all that much. We could even have become friends, I thought. I'd tell her about all the crazy shit that people call about at work and the shit that goes on where I live and she would understand. She would get it. But then I kept thinking back to that guy who went to her place. It was driving me crazy not knowing *exactly* what was going on there.

I got a call from some idiot in Georgia who didn't like the fact that there was a section of New Age books in the store. "As far as I'm concerned, that's just promoting witchcraft. That's what you're doing, you know. You're promoting witchcraft."

"I'm sorry that you feel that way, ma'am. That's really not our intention."

"Oh, it's not?! Then what would you call it?"

"Well ma'am, we aren't trying to promote any particular theme or genre. We're not favoring one over another. As you know, we have various displays throughout the store."

"Yes, but children, young children, easily get to the books on display at this table and think that because Astor House Books is promoting it, then it's okay to read. Before you know it, they're going to be buying more books on witchcraft and trying to practice it themselves and you know what that leads to? Devil worship and suicide, that's what!"

"I understand your concerns, ma'am and I will make sure to voice your opinion."

"Are you going to take down the display?"

"No ma'am, I'm afraid not. Our displays change virtually on a weekly basis and so it will eventually come down, but for the time being, it's scheduled to remain there for another three weeks."

"Another three weeks! Do you know what that could do to a child?! Is anyone up there thinking about the children?!"

"We're very concerned about our younger customers, ma'am. We just ask that parents or guardians exercise caution when they are in our stores with minors."

"Well, we can't keep an eye on them every minute."

"Neither can we."

"What did you say?!"

I hadn't even realized what I had said until it too late. "What I meant to say, ma'am, was that uh…we certainly…um, understand your concern about shopping in our stores with children and…and we understand your concerns about some of our displays. However, um…we do uh, have a strict no censorship policy. We have gotten complaints from various people over the things that we sell in our stores and as we…respect the choices that customers make about the things they buy and where they buy them, we just ask that our customers respect our decision to sell any and all titles that are currently in print."

"Well! Since you understand the concept of decisions so much, I'm just going to decide not to buy any more books at Astor House and I'm going to tell everyone I know of to do the same!" Click. It was the first time that something like that had happened to me. In all the years I had been doing that job, I never once slipped or broke protocol like that and I was lucky that the customer hadn't asked to be transferred to Captain Marvel. I have to admit, it kind of felt good.

After the experience I had with Elsa over the weekend, I really felt like things were turning around for me. I only saw her once on the train that week, but she hadn't seen me though. I made sure to stay well hidden in the next car, and I visited her place almost every night. It was the last time, however, where I almost got caught.

The whole situation with that guy kept creeping up on me and I didn't like it. I wanted to see what else I could find in her apartment that might give me more information, so I would watch her through her window as she slept most nights. The guy hadn't been back again as far as I saw so I started to think that maybe they were through with whatever it was they had been…doing. After work, I would have a quick dinner at home, get dressed and head over to Elsa's. Sometimes, I'd have to stay by the trash and just stare at her windows because the people on the first or second floors refused to go to bed early.

I saw her leave one Friday night at around 9. She was dressed in a short sleeve black and white striped top with a black skirt and wedge heels. Checking her purse for her cell phone, she quickly spoke with someone and turned to walk up to the other avenue. As I followed her, I began wondering if she was going to meet up with someone, specifically him – whoever *he* was. When she got to the avenue, however, she crossed the street and immediately went into the Beer Garden that was on the corner. On summer nights, they opened up their backyard and sometimes they had a band. That night, I saw there was a large crowd in the back and there were people setting up instruments on stage. Figuring she would be there for a while, I went back to her building, through the alley and up the fire escape.

I thought there would be some kind of evidence I could find in her apartment as to what was going on with this man and I crawled inside her bedroom window. When I got to the kitchen, I noticed there were a couple of dishes and a pan in the sink, but aside from that everything else looked normal. There was some mail on the dining room table and she had since replaced the yellow tulips with some white Calla lilies. As I got to the bar, however, I noticed there were two empty glasses that had been used, only one of which had a lipstick mark.

Immediately, I went back to her bedroom and looked around. Sifting through her garbage can by the desk, I found some tissues, eyeliner pencil shavings and some crumbled receipts from the dry cleaner. Her laptop was open and so I thought I'd try to check her email, but unfortunately, she had signed out and there was no way I could access her account. Frustrated, I went back to the sitting room and examined the glass closely. I don't know what I was looking for exactly, but I wasn't thinking very clearly. If I had been, I might have heard her in the hallway *before* she turned her key in the lock.

Luckily, I hadn't turned on any lights so she didn't suspect anything when she walked in the door. I had crouched down behind the bar. It may not have been the safest place to hide, but my options were limited and I it wasn't like I could just climb out of the third floor window onto Astoria Boulevard. She was speaking with someone when she came in and closed the door. "…really, I'm sorry. I'm just not feeling up to it tonight. I thought once I got there that I could relax and forget about things, but I just want to be home in bed." She was alone and was on her cell. When she made her way to the back of the apartment, though, I realized that I had left the window open.

I thought that my only chance to leave was if she went to the bathroom and then I could go through the front door, which was closest. But I didn't want to run the risk of her finding the window open, so I thought if she did go to the bathroom, I could sneak past, climb out and shut it before she got there. "Thanks hun, I really appreciate you trying to make me feel better. I'll snap out of it eventually. Guess I just miss him already," she said. *"Miss who?"* I thought. It had to be that guy from the other time. She *missed* him?!

"Look, how about if I give you a call tomorrow, okay? No, I just…I know, I know. Thanks again. No, I'm just going to go to bed. I'm tired and I want to wake up early and go to the gym." She laughed at something that whoever she was talking to said, poured herself something to drink in the kitchen and thanked them again. "I'll talk to you tomorrow, sweetie. Thanks again." I wanted to peek around the bar to see what she was doing, but then I heard her put the glass down and walk toward her room. Slowly, I inched toward the edge of the bar and saw her turn on the light in her room and sit on her bed. After taking off her shoes, she sat there and stared at the floor. Even as sad as she seemed to be at that moment, she still looked so beautiful. All I wanted to do was take her in my arms and hold her for the rest of the night, telling her in between our heated kisses that everything would be okay. I wanted to tell her that I would take care of her and that I wouldn't let anything make her sad again.

She shook her head suddenly and then got up and went to the bathroom. I had to chance going to her room, as she hadn't noticed that the window was open. Quickly, but quietly, I made my way back to her room. As I passed the kitchen, I noticed that it looked like she had used the same glass that I had the time. I think I may have smiled about this while I got to the window. Just as I was about to step onto the fire escape, I saw she had left her cell phone on her nightstand. My heart was pounding and I knew I had to leave before she came out but I also thought about the opportunity. When else would I be able to have access to her cell and maybe find out a little more about what she was going through? Carefully, I went to her nightstand and turned her phone on. There was a screen saver of Marilyn Monroe and just as I swiped it, she received a text message. Before I could see who it was from, I heard the toilet flush and the faucet had been turned on. Looking at the bathroom door, I realized that I wouldn't have time to get through the window and close it behind me before being spotted. And I also couldn't walk past the bathroom to leave through the front door because she would see and hear me as well. The closet was out of the question because there simply wasn't enough room. I heard the water stop and out of panic, I dropped the phone when another text message arrived.

The bathroom door swung open and after she turned off the light, she walked into her room. After she looked in the mirror, she took off her contacts and rubbed her eyes. She let her skirt drop to the floor, took her shirt off, then her bra, and left them all in a pile next to the bed. Afterwards, she put on a pair of black shorts and a pink t-shirt. While rubbing some lotion on her hands and elbows, she noticed that the window was open. Taking a look outside, she leaned over, closed the window and made sure that she locked it. When she went back to her desk, she fished out a sleeping mask and sat on the bed. Before she laid down, however, she noticed that her cell phone was not on the nightstand where she had left it and stood up to look around.

It lay a few feet away from me, on the other side of the nightstand. She spotted it quickly, picked it up, checked it, and laid down in bed after she responded to whoever had texted. As I lay on the floor, underneath her bed, I heard the box-spring move slightly as she adjusted herself for the night.

It took about fifteen minutes for her to fall asleep, but I hadn't moved for what felt like an hour. All that time, I heard my heart beat a mile a minute and eventually, I heard the sound of her heaving breathing. The apartment was completely dark except for the yellow lights of the street lamps outside. Slowly, I made my way from under her bed as soon as I thought enough time had passed and she seemed to be in a deep sleep. Little by little, I moved toward the wall with the window. My plan was to quietly unlatch the window and make my way back to the alley. That way, I could leave the window unlocked for next time.

Peering from the side of her bed, I saw that she was on her side, away from the wall. She had started to snore softly and I couldn't help but smile. When I crawled out from under the bed and made my way to the window, I gently unlocked it and slowly opened it just enough to get through, wincing at every creak I thought for sure would give me away. Just as I was getting ready to climb out, I looked at her and realized that it was the perfect opportunity to get a picture of her sleeping. I wanted to capture that moment and instantly I felt myself getting excited at the thought. She shifted in bed a little as I took out my cell and got ready to take one more picture of her. For a second, or maybe several minutes I'm not really sure, I stood there and stared at her sleeping. It was almost perfect, that moment; just she and I, finally alone. The rest of the world outside seemed to disappear as I moved closer to her. Even though the window was open and it was a beautiful, warm summer night, the only thing I heard was her breathing softly. She was loosely covered in her blanket, and although I would have loved to have felt what that was like, I refrained from touching her. I understood at that moment what I had been missing all my life and as I watched her delicate face lay peacefully on her pillow, all I thought about was joining her. Hell, I would have sold my soul to have been able to wrap myself up with her at that moment forever. *"I could make you happy,"* I thought, or I may have whispered it, I can't remember. Standing next to her bed, I steadied the cell and realized how lucky I was that she was wearing a sleeping mask – she wouldn't be able to see the flash. She moved again slightly when I took the first shot and I wondered for a minute if she had woken up. When I heard her gentle snoring, though, I knew I was safe. After I took another one, I leaned over her and blew her a kiss before leaving.

As soon as I got home, I turned on a playlist of songs I had put together on my computer and uploaded the pictures I had taken.

James Blunt's, *You're Beautiful*, came on and I smiled when I saw how perfect the images had come out. Carefully, I placed them on the wall next to the others. When I was done, I made some iced tea and while the next few songs played, I sat crossed-legged on the floor and looked up at her in wonder. A drop of water fell from the glass onto my leg and even though at that moment I didn't remember having taken my clothes off, the water felt good against my skin. I put the glass down and walked up to the wall. "Perfect," I said, slowly running my hand across all the pictures. Some were the same, but I had also changed the images on a few and there was one, the one from the restaurant, where I had photo-shopped myself sitting next to her. It had taken some time to get it right, but once I did, I printed it out and put it on a frame next to my computer. We looked like such a great couple.

Chapter Eighteen

I hadn't seen her at all that weekend. When I went over on Saturday and Sunday, not only was she not home, but she had locked the window. The rest of that week was the same story. Even after I waited around the train platform, or Hoyt Park, it seemed like she had suddenly vanished. And the fact that I couldn't get into her apartment added to my frustration. I thought that maybe she gone away on vacation, which was fine, but I wondered if *he* had gone with her. Despite the fact that he was faceless to me, I found it hard to block the image of the two of them together. Whenever I thought of them wrapped up in bed, sharing a kiss, sharing each other, it would drive me crazy to the point where a car almost hit Cherry as I walked her one night.

The following Friday, some people from our floor had gotten together in the break-room to cut a cake for Brian. Even though he wouldn't be officially through until 4, George didn't want him handling anything since he wouldn't be able to follow up with anyone after that day. George led us all in a rendition of "For He's a

Jolly Good Fellow," the obligatory send off tune whenever anyone had a birthday or left the company. It was supposed to symbolize company unity and no-hard-feelings all at once. Whatever. At least they had a decent cake.

Afterward, each of us took turns saying goodbye before we went back to work. After Floyd told Brian how much he'd miss him, it was my turn. "Good working with you," I said.
"Same here. Take of yourself. Don't let them get to you," he smiled.

I hadn't seen her since in a week's time and I left as soon as I was done for the day. Sure enough, that day my timing was perfect and I saw her get on at 59th. She smiled when she saw me and said hello when I walked over. She had said hello *and* my name. "Hello, Everest." She remembered! That time, she remembered. She looked great, too. Dress down Fridays obviously did not apply at her job. She had on a red jacket over a black dress that stayed just above her knees. Even after a day of shuffling papers, her perfume was still in the air around her.

"We keep bumping into each other, lately," she said. "I'm going to start to think that I'm being followed." I laughed and glanced around the car. "How are you?" she asked. Goddamn it her voice was soft, she sounded so much better than last Friday when she was upset.

"Not bad, thanks. How are you?"

"Okay. Thank God it's Friday, huh?"

"Yeah, definitely. I know what you mean. That's so true," I said, trying to sound relaxed.

"You always get out of work at this time?"

"Um, more or less. Sometimes I have to stay later, but usually, um…yeah. You?"

"Same. Sometimes I have to stay late but I try to get out on time. You can only take work for so long, you know?" she smiled.

"So what do you do?" she asked, finally. The train had come out of the tunnel and we would get to Queensboro Plaza in a few moments. People would be getting off and I wouldn't be pressed up against her, unfortunately. "I…work in customer service. For a bookchain."

"Oh really? Which one?"

"Astor House Books."

"Oh yeah, they have some nice stores."

"Yeah. Are you a reader?"

"A book a week."

"Really?"

"Yes, I get lost in books, really. Sometimes I'll go into a Barnes & Noble, or Astor House Books, excuse me," she laughed, "and just spend hours going through the aisles."

"I know what you mean."

"It must be great to work there. Do you get many customer service issues?"

"Um, well sometimes, you know? It depends."

"People can be pretty demanding sometimes, huh?"

"Yes. Yes, they can be."

When people got off at the Plaza, she moved back a little and got some breathing space. Some guy had gotten up from the seat and she offered it to me. Even though I kept offering it to her, she wouldn't take it at first. She finally took it and even though I tried not to look, I couldn't help it and snuck a glance at her legs. As she

adjusted herself, though, just on the inside of her right thigh, I saw a

small bruise. It could easily have been missed, but there it was – a

circular black and blue on her otherwise perfect, white thigh. She

finished getting settled and straightened out her skirt a little further

down, which hid the mark. It had been there long enough for me to

have seen it though, and it hadn't looked like she had noticed me

looking. It looked like the kind of mark that you'd get if someone

were to…grab you really hard. At the next station, a pregnant

woman got on and she immediately got up and offered her the seat.

A few minutes after that, Ben walked through the connecting

doors and made his usual introductions. When he walked up to us, I

dug in my pocket and gave him a dollar and watched her do the

same. "Thank you both so much. And just look at those smiles. I

always say I get my best smiles on this train." It may have been my

imagination, but I thought I saw her blush a little. I still couldn't see

past her sunglasses, but at that point I didn't care. It was enough for

me that I was there, talking to her, and breathing in her perfume.

"So, uh, been to Lee's lately?" I asked.

"No, not recently. Not since that last time."

"They have pretty good food there."

"Yeah, their General Tso's is great."

"So you're a fan of Chinese food, huh? Ever go to China Garden on 21st?"

"Never heard of it. China Garden? 21st and what?"

"It's on 21st Street, just off the Queensborough Bridge."

"Oh, no. I've never been there." Of course she had never been there. She didn't look like the type of woman who ever needed to go to my part of Astoria. "Good food?"

"Yeah, they're okay. I mean, you know, not as good as Lee's, but they're okay."

"I'll have to remember that."

She was bored, I could tell. I remember thinking, *"How could I expect to be friends with her if I couldn't even keep up my end of a decent conversation?"* "So what's it like? Being a para-legal, I mean."

"It's okay. To be honest, I really haven't been doing it that long."

"That doesn't surprise me."

"Why do you say that?"

"Well, you look like you only just got out of college, so I can't imagine that you have that much experience with anything in the job market."

"That's sweet, but you're way off on that one," she laughed.

"Way off? Aw, come on, I don't think that I could be that way off."

"Believe me, I'm probably older than you are."

"You think so?"

"In all probability, yes."

"Well, I was taught never to ask a woman how old she is, so I'll guess I'll never know."

"Whoever taught you that was very, very smart. But, there's nothing wrong with me asking you how old you are, so if you tell me, I'll tell you whether or not I'm older."

"Ah, the ol' double standard, huh?"

"Sometimes it works to our advantage."

"That's true."

"So?"

"So what?"

"How old are you?"

"Oh, I'm 30."

"I'm older."

"Really?"

"Afraid so," she smiled.

"You've got to be kidding."

"Believe me, I wish that I were."

"Well, you certainly don't look it. I mean, not in the least."

"Thanks. You're very sweet."

Things couldn't have gone better, until we got to Astoria Boulevard. I knew that I would have to good-bye because I couldn't get off at her stop; it would look too suspicious. We were having such a great time! It wasn't fair that I had to say goodbye to her and not hear from her again until I had arranged another "accidental" meeting on the train, I thought. *"Even then,"* I thought, *"how many of these could actually get away with before she suspected that I was rigging all of them?"* I couldn't keep bumping into her at the store either, could I? That's when I thought that I would just ask her to get a cup of coffee. A simple cup of coffee. That would be safe.

The N was coming up fast on Astoria Boulevard, I saw the familiar rooftops. "Listen, I uh…I know that we uh…we uh, don't really…know each other…that well, but uh, I was…I was just wondering if maybe -" the train stopped suddenly in-between stations. I took it as a sign, it was the perfect opportunity. "Maybe we could…you wanna get some coffee? If you like coffee, I mean? Do you…drink coffee?"

She looked at me, smiled and then looked at the floor. I couldn't tell if maybe she was being coy? God, it looked like she was going to say yes. What the hell was I going to do if she said yes? I had to stay cool and relaxed. I didn't want to let on how much it would have meant to me if she said yes. There were so many places that I thought I could take her too if she said yes. There were Greek, Italian, Spanish, Romanian, Croatian places, all which were within walking distance from her place. She was sure to like one of them. I started to wonder which one I would take her to because it had to be just right. It couldn't be too romantic or anything like that. Still, it had to have just the right kind of atmosphere. She looked like I had caught her totally off guard. That had to be cool, right? Women like it when guys catch them off guard, don't they? It's part of that whole spontaneity thing. Almost like sweeping her off her feet and all that. At least, she was still smiling so that's what I thought. I remember standing there, trying to think of something really witty to say after she accepted my invitation. Nothing came to mind, but I figured something would after she would say yes.

"Thanks, but I can't this time."

She probably noticed the look on my face because as soon as she turned me down, she immediately apologized. She apologized. I told her that it was okay and that she didn't have to be sorry, that I understood. "It's just that I already have plans for tonight, you know?"

"Sure. No really, I understand," I said. The train had started moving and we pulled into the station. "Actually-"

"Maybe some other time, though," she said.

"Yeah. Uh, that sounds...sounds great." The train stopped hard and she grabbed my arm to steady herself.

"God, where do they learn to drive these things," she said. I think I smiled. "Well, it was nice seeing you again Everest," she mumbled as she made her way to the platform.

Already had plans. Hearing that was like being smacked awake. Already had plans. The bus ride home was quiet and I felt like people were looking at me. She already had plans. I tried not to look at anyone but at one point I looked up from the floor and it seemed like people were fucking smiling at me! My stomach turned and I looked back down at the floor. Plans. Goddamn plans. Yeah, she had *plans* alright. She had plans with…that guy, I was sure of it! She had plans with that guy who was with her in her apartment. The one who had grabbed her so hard he had left a fucking mark on her and she was going to meet with him again?! What the hell kind of fucking plans were those?!

I don't remember when I got home, but I remember that my apartment seemed deathly silent. I lost track of how long I had stood in the middle of the room, staring at the wall where her pictures were. It really wasn't fucking fair. It wasn't fair! Not the fact that she had plans, Jesus, almost everybody has *plans*. It was the fact that she had plans with him. Who the fuck was he? Did he think about her the way I did? Did he go out almost every night just to try and take her picture so that he could look at her, so that he could feel better whenever things got to be too much? What the hell did he do for her? Besides marking up that perfect body, I mean. All I saw was him going over and drawing the shades. What the hell was he doing? He was using her! That's what it was, he was using her. Using her to fill his lust like every other fucking guy that looked at her on the train. He was using her to fill some bottomless void that he couldn't ever fill in his regular life because it was so fucking mundane and empty. That's what he was doing! He couldn't fill it with anything else, so he was trying to fill it by using someone who was real, someone who was good, someone who was generous and kind, someone who was better than the usual trash he violated. She was someone who didn't wince away when someone like Ben walked through the train looking for something to eat. She was someone who said hello to people when she saw them on the street, and held doors open for old people. She was someone who knew how hard it was to wake up every morning and go to a job that just asked for more and more from you and no matter how much you gave, it would never be enough. Just like him! Of course, she was so good that she didn't see it. She wouldn't report his abuse to anyone because she was probably trying to help him! She didn't see him for what he really was, a vampire. She couldn't comprehend that there were vampires like him all over the place, dying to sink themselves into her and drain her. She just saw him as a pathetic, lost soul that she could try to bring back by being as kind and giving as possible. Maybe she figured that if she yielded all her love and her body and her mind to him that he'd see something in her that would make him change. He wouldn't, of course. He'd just keep coming back for more. He'd come back again and again and again, leaving more marks on her. And they'd probably get bigger each and every time. He wouldn't be happy until he had sucked all that goodness out of her. He wouldn't be happy until he had possessed her and then when he was done with her, after he'd broken her, after he'd totally spent and wasted every drop of sick fucking fluid inside himself, he'd just toss her away and never give another moment's thought that he'd just buried one of the only decent people left in the world. One of the few people that everyone else should aspire to be like. That motherfucker would just keep coming back and he would draw those shades over and over again until he was satisfied. Until she had nothing else to give.

The next thing I knew, I was out on the street and I was so pissed that I almost got to Astoria Park without realizing it. I had to see her. I had to see if those plans that she mentioned involved something more than just drawing the goddamn shades again! While I walked, I pulled out my cell and looked at the shot I had of her on the platform of Astoria Boulevard. The way she looked, the way her hair was set, everything was captured in that one instant and I had her. I had her there. It was the perfect shot. I realized that no matter where I looked at it, sitting at my desk or under a streetlight, it had the same affect on me. As mad as I was, it still calmed me. At least, a little.

As I got to the corner of 21st Street and 26th Avenue, right in front of the old Irish Famine Cemetery, I heard somebody yell out "Please!" When I looked down 26th, I saw a young girl who was trying to get away from this guy in a blue Chevy Nova. His arm was sticking out the passenger window and held on to her wrist. Whoever was in the driver's seat was inching the car up a little at a time to make her keep up with them. She was a young black girl in a pair of tight, cut-off jeans and black thick-soled shoes. She had a rainbow colored top and her hair was pulled back into a ponytail. Even from where I was stood, I saw the bright pink lipstick she caked on and even anyone could see that she didn't want any part of those guys in the car.

I was going to walk away. Seriously, I was going to keep walking over to Elsa's. After all, that was the reason I went out. I looked at my watch and saw that it was after eleven. Lately it had seemed like whenever I checked the time, it was like I'd lost hours. The Nova screeched its tires and I looked up sharply.

Elsa was probably a million miles away. Even if that bastard hadn't taken her out of the apartment, she was still a million miles away from that situation. I wondered, *"What would she say about it? What would she say about something like this?"* The guy in the car pulled her toward him and she fell. He wouldn't let go of her wrist and didn't seem to care about that he was hurting her!

"Are you okay?" I called out as I walked toward her. She looked up at me and squinted. "Are you okay?" I asked again. The car's taillights went from red, to reverse white and back to red. They had put it in park. The driver got out and walked around to the sidewalk. "What fuckin' bidne is it ah yours?" He stood in the street, right in the dried up gutter, with a gray Mets jersey and navy blue jeans that hung low so everybody could see that he wore gray boxers. He was a short, stocky, Hispanic kid with a black tribal tattoo on his left forearm. It apparently ran up his arm and stopped just under his right ear. His bald head made him look like an escaped mental patient. Meanwhile, the guy in the passenger's seat had let go of the girl and opened the door as well. He was a tall black guy with long dreads and a Bob Marley tie-dye tee shirt untucked over a pair of black leather pants. The girl had backed up against the doorway of a building next to the cemetery and the guy just stood by the car, sizing me up.

"S'up bitch? S'up bitch, you deaf? Ha? You deaf or what, muthafuckah?!" the bald guy took a step toward me. I looked at the girl and she just stood there, trying to figure out what the hell was going on. That made two of us. "Check it out, Jimmy, we got us fuckin' Batman ovah here," he said. Jimmy stayed by the car and didn't say anything. He figured he'd let his driver try and figure out what was going before making a move. "S'up, Batman?! You gonna do sunthin', huh? You gonna do sunthin? Watcha gonna do? Watcha gonna do, Batman?! You a cop?"

"No, I'm not." The minute I had said it, I wondered how smart it was to admit that I wasn't a cop just then. Jimmy walked right up to me.

He stood about two feet away from me and looked me up and down. His friend kept shifting his weight and taking a step forward, then back, forward and then back again. "You know this girl?" he asked. I shook my head. "So why don't you mind your own fuckin' business bitch?!" and he clocked me with a right across the face. I went down like a rock.

Not content with letting Jimmy have all the fun, the bald guy came up and kicked me in the stomach. "Yo, Charlene. You sure you don't know this…asshole?"

"Baby, I aint never seent him before."

"You sure?!"

"Baby, I swear. I swear, baby, I don't know who the fuck he is."

Jimmy looked around and kicked me a couple of times, catching me in the head with one of his boots. His friend leaned me on my side and nailed me dead in the face.

Right after that, they started going through my pockets. I tried to grab their hands, but kept getting kicked. One of them got my wallet and when the other felt my cell, he tried to take it out of my pocket. "No!" I yelled and struggled to get away. I didn't care about the phone as I did about the pictures of Elsa that I had saved. If they kept kicking and hitting me, eventually they'd get the phone. They would take her from me. That's when I started to feel a rage build up from the pit of my stomach, even though it ached from the kicks. *"These bastards are going to take her from me!"* I thought. Suddenly, I realized that it was possible that some guy already had taken her from me. And just like my mother, pictures would be all that I'd have left. Images of her on the train ran through my mind and then all I saw was the bruise on her leg. More and more, I felt the pressure build up within me as I thought about how some worthless piece of shit, like the two that were beating me, had hurt her. Nobody understood what a crime that was, hurting her. I thought about how they were all alike, the two that were trying to rob me, the guy that hurt her and all those people who called the company every day to complain about something. They were all trying to drown me in their own pathetic, worthless wants and selfishness. By then I felt numb, everything except the anger had left my body and all I could think about was hurting the two bastards that beat me. Somehow between the cursing and the kicking and grabbing, I made it to the curb where I found an open 40 ounce bottle of Old English half filled with what smelled like piss. Quickly taking it in my hands, I threw it at them and caught one on the side of the head. "SON OF A BITCH!" yelled the bald guy, as the bottle smashed against Jimmy's head, knocking him to the ground. The bald guy backed off for a minute and it was all I needed to punch him in the balls as I stood up. Jimmy seemed unconscious and I could see that his head was covered with blood. Curled up into a ball next to him, the bald guy groaned on the sidewalk.

My mouth was bleeding and I spat it at them. Charlene seemed too scared to move and I looked at her for a second before saying anything. "ARE YOU OKAY?!" I screamed and spit in her direction before I walked away. When I made it to the corner, I turned and saw Charlene on her phone and the bald guy had just managed to sit up.

A few blocks later, the pain got worse. Suddenly, I felt like throwing up. I made it a few steps more and then sat against a building. The nausea had started to fade, but my body still hurt like hell. I slowly looked up at the night sky and saw that there were stars out, not a lot, but there were a few here and there. A car drove past and I heard some people walk past me. These people had come out of the building and at least looked at me sitting there before they walked off.

I don't know how long I was there before somebody finally came up and said something. Truth of the matter was that I was afraid to move. My tongue played with this chipped front tooth and I kind of wondered what the hell happened to the missing piece. It was quite possible that I had swallowed it. Thinking about that just reminded me of the whole assault and that made me feel like throwing up again, so I just concentrated on the stars. I sort of remember someone with a thick Indian accent that asked if I was okay. My head pounded even more than it had before, but at least I still had the pictures of her. Whoever it was asked me again if I was okay. When

I didn't answer, I felt their hands on me, trying to snap me out of it.

"I'm...tired," I said. Whispered, actually. He leaned in and asked

me to repeat what I said and even though I tried, I couldn't form the

words. I was screaming them inside, though. I even felt it in the

blood that was drying up on my face. "I'm tired," I finally managed.

Chapter Nineteen

Eventually, the cops showed up and they called an ambulance. They kept asking me all kinds of stupid questions. My name, my address, what I was doing there, what happened, could I describe whoever had hit me, that kind of thing. I didn't answer them right away. The first thing out of my mouth was that I wanted to go. I didn't tell them where, I just told them that I wanted to go. "We can't let you go, sir. You've got to go to the hospital and get checked out," one of the EMS guys said. "Why don't you just tell us your name, okay? How about it? Just your name? Let's start from there."

"E…Everest."

"What?"

"Everest. Everest Porter."

"Everest Porter. That's your name?" When I nodded, he asked me where I lived and I gave him my address. Then he asked me if I had any family and I said no. "Well, is there anyone that you want us to call?"

Of course there was. Of course there was someone I wanted to call. The problem was that not only did I not have her phone number but she was probably too busy with her...plans, with him. The one who shut out the rest of the world so that he could subject to her to whatever sick sexual cravings he had. Of course I wanted to call her. I wanted to do more than that. I wanted to go to her and tell her how I felt. I wanted to take her in my arms and swing her around like they did in the movies and watch her laugh and smile and see her eyes finally look into mine and say, "Everest. Everest, you're here. Everything will be okay."

Oddly enough, it was quiet at the hospital. As quiet as hospital ERs can be anyway. They finished taking down all of my information and contacted my insurance company. I gave the cops a description of Jimmy and the other guy. They wanted to know why I decided to butt in on something like that. I just shrugged my shoulders. How do you answer that?

There was no internal bleeding and no broken bones. There was no concussion, but they wanted to keep me overnight anyway, just for observation. I wanted to leave, still hoping that I could maybe get to her building on time to see her, even if it was just once. Even if it was before the…shades were drawn. I wanted to leave. It's just that I felt so tired all of a sudden, as if I hadn't slept in nights. Maybe it was the aftereffect of the beating and the adrenaline and all that, but I really couldn't keep my eyes open.

She was in my dream that night. We were standing on top of her building and the sun was going down, only it wasn't Astoria. It was someplace warm and nice and clean. There were no other buildings around or anyone else for that matter. It was just me and her. She was smiling and wearing this yellow sundress with white sandals. I was stroking her hair and she closed her eyes and whispered something, but I couldn't make out what she was saying. It didn't matter, though, that I couldn't figure out what she had said. It still made me feel good just to hear that she said something, just to be around her. Then I leaned in closer and she repeated whatever it was she had said before but I still couldn't make it out. I laughed and drew her in closer so I could wrap my arm around her waist. She put her hands on my shoulders and kissed me while the sun went down. It got black all around us suddenly, though, and somehow I lost her and saw that I was standing by myself. The wind had kicked up and there was this constant buzzing all around me, like a thousand voices all talking at the same time. I ran across the roof of her building, but I couldn't find her. Finally, I looked over the edge. She stood in front of her building, laughing. The buzzing was getting louder and I made out a few words here and there from a bunch of different voices. "Disgusting," "Discount," "Coffee," "Music." The pitch would rise and fall suddenly and when I looked at her again, I saw that the sundress was gone and she was covered in bruises. When I squinted, I saw that she hadn't been laughing at all. She was crying and her bruises had all turned to welts. I reached down to her and when she looked at me, everything got quiet. It was like she cut through all the noise and the wind just stopped out of nowhere and somehow, I was able to reach down to her and she looked right at me and whispered, "Bye."

When I woke up it was after 3 AM. I was alone except for the occasional nurse that walked by. One of them checked in on me and took my blood pressure. "How are you feeling?" she asked in a light Trinidadian accent.

"Okay."

"That's good. Tomorrow morning, if everything is okay, you can go home."

"I can't -"

"You can't?" I shook my head. "Why can't you?" she asked. Closing my eyes, I grunted once and farted. She undid the blood pressure unit and left. About a half hour later, I turned my head and eventually went back to sleep.

By the time I was discharged the next day, it was after two in the afternoon. The thought of taking the bus back to my apartment made me feel exhausted, so I came up with the idea to ask Steve for a ride. I dug through my wallet and after I found his card, I called him. Melissa answered, she had just gotten back from shopping.

"You must be psychic," she said, "I'm just walking through the door."

"Sorry to bother you."

"No, it's okay, no bother. How are you?"

"I'm fine, thanks. Listen, is Steve home by any chance?"

"Um…I don't think so. Let me see." She walked around the apartment, looking for traces of him while I stayed on the line. "No, sorry. He's not home yet. He did say that he was going to the office this morning, did you try there?"

"No," I grimaced, realizing that I should've tried there first. "No."

"Well, do you have the number?"

"Yeah, I got it. Thanks Melissa. I'll just…I'll try again later."

"You sure? He's probably still there if you want to call him. His office has an 800 number if you're out of change or something."

"It does?"

"Yeah." She gave me the number and told me that I could find his extension after punching in his last name through the auto-directory.

"Thanks Melissa."

"Anytime. You sure you're okay? You sound…kind of out of it."

"Yeah, I'm fine, thanks. Really, don't worry. I'll give Steve a call. Thanks again for the number. I'll try to catch him before he goes home."

"Okay. Talk to you soon."

The clock on the wall over the reception desk read 2:25. I hoped to still catch him. The auto-directory immediately connected me to his extension but I just got his voicemail. I didn't leave a message. That's when I decided to just get some money out of the ATM and take a taxi home.

Hilda and Cherry were sitting outside the building when the cab pulled up. After paying the fare, I slowly walked toward the building. Her jaw dropped open when she saw me and Cherry immediately came over. "Oh sweet Lord! What on earth happened to you?!" After telling her that I got jumped the previous night trying to help someone, she helped me inside and into my apartment. "Are you hungry?" she asked, easing me on the couch.

"No. No, not hungry."

"Thirsty? Can I get you anything?"

"No." She went into the bedroom, brought out a pillow and put it under my head. "You sure you wouldn't be more comfortable on your own bed?"

"No. This is fine. I've been in a bed all night."

"Yeah but that was one of those hospital beds. There's nothing like your own mattress when you're feeling banged up."

"This is fine. Thanks, Hilda." Hobbling across the room, she opened the window a little. "Fresh air will help you feel better," she said.

"I got the shit kicked out of me for trying to be a nice guy. I don't think fresh air is gonna help me feel any better." My answer startled her, and I realized that I had sounded harsher than I had intended, so I apologized and told her the whole story.

"You did the right thing," she pulled open the curtains and pulled a chair over to the sofa. "How were you supposed to know that the girl wasn't worth it?"

"Oh come on, Hilda, I deal with people everyday. All sorts, all types. Liars, thieves, con artists, perverts. There's rarely a call that comes through that doesn't make me wonder if there's a decent person left in the world." She looked down at the floor and straightened her glasses. "Present company not included, of course," I said and she smiled. Cherry laid next to me and tried to lick my face.

"Listen, I know how it can get sometimes when you're dealing with those kinds of people all day, but you can't let it touch you inside. Those people, they're not <u>all</u> people. They're just the people you get paid to deal with, that's all. It's nothing personal, so don't take it personally. When they call you, they don't see or hear a person. They're seeing a big, rich company, that's all. That's who they're talking to, not you. So don't give them the satisfaction of knowing that they got under your skin. You keep on being you because you're a nice person. The world needs nice people. What you did for that girl, that was very brave, Everest. Not many people would've done that. But something inside you, something told you to try and help her and you did. Ok, so it didn't turn out for the best, but that's all on them, Everest, not you. Don't let that sour you on people. Don't let your job sour you on people. That's how hate starts. World's got enough of that."

Hilda lost her husband during the Trade Center attack. He was one of the security guards that stayed behind to help other people get out. She lost one of her sons in the Persian Gulf War. If anybody had a reason to be sour it was Hilda. *"How the hell does she do it?"* I wondered.

"Huh? I didn't hear you," she said. I must have said that out-loud again.

"Nothing," I lied. I kind of wanted her to leave. For one thing, I was starting to get a headache and for another, I just didn't want to hear any of that shit. So the world had enough hate, well, we brought it on ourselves. If the people that I talked to at work and the asshole who was manhandling Elsa were reflective of the type of society that we lived in, then it was no wonder that I sounded sour on people. It was no wonder that I couldn't look at any of these fucking people without wanting to smash their faces in. Especially when I found one of the few truly pure people left in the world with some guy whose only intent was to feed his lust and pervert her into the same type of jaded slime that he saw in the mirror everyday.

She insisted on making dinner before she left and by the time she was done, the stew she had thrown together with whatever the hell I was growing in the fridge smelled pretty good. I wasn't really hungry, but just to make her happy I ate two bowls while we watched some TV. "Now don't you think twice about calling me if you need something in the middle of the night. I don't care what time it is, you just call me," she said as she walked toward the door, Cherry in tow.

"I will. Thanks again for everything, Hilda."

"Don't you worry about that, just concentrate on getting better. And don't worry about walking Cherry, I'll take care of that. You sure that's enough, by the way? You need more?"

"No, thanks. Really, you gave me more than enough."

"Okay then. And you sure you won't change your mind about staying at my apartment?"

"Thanks, Hilda. I'm...really, I'm fine here. I just want to rest."

"Okay, Everest. Have a good night, then."

I thought more and more about what Hilda had said. It got darker outside and pretty soon, the only light in the room was coming off the TV. The 10 O'clock news came on and Kaity Tong was talking about the latest developments in Iraq. I turned it off after a few minutes and just stared at the ceiling until my eyes got used to the dark. It's funny how your own place looks different at night, almost like a different apartment. I guess everything is different when there are no lights on and things seemed like different colors. Shadows give everyday items an unfamiliar look. But then you get other things that don't change, like the sounds and smells. It's at that moment when you see that nothing's different, nothing's changed. You were still in the same fucking apartment, listening to the same fucking people, going to the same fucking job, and stuck in the same fucking rut you've seemingly always been in. But according to Hilda, you're not supposed to sour.

Not sour?! I turned on my side and the pain in my back told me that that wasn't a good idea. Downstairs in the courtyard, the kids were out. Rap music, salsa, all mixed into one uneven rhythm. Simone was probably fucking a John in her apartment. Brian was probably out getting drunk to celebrate the last of those phone calls he'd ever have to take. Sofia was checking her Lotto numbers, in the hopes that she wouldn't actually have to go into work on Monday. Captain Marvel was probably having dinner at some trendy restaurant with the wife while the nanny watched his kids. Floyd was most likely asleep.

At some point during the night, I wound up in bed and stayed there for the rest of the weekend. I wanted to go out to Elsa's, but there was no way my body was having any of that. After I took a shower, I had some of Hilda's stew again. She and Cherry came by and stayed for a couple of hours on Saturday and Sunday. As I thanked her, I tried not to sound too irritated. After all, she made dinner for me over the weekend and was nice enough to try to keep me company. Still, I couldn't help it. She was one of those people that just...fucking pissed me off. Not because of anything specific, but just because she always seemed to have all the Goddamn answers. That was really annoying. If she was so fucking smart, then why the hell did she live in that shithole?!

I called out sick on Monday. Honestly, I don't think George believed me when I told him what happened, but I didn't care. Besides, he would see on Tuesday. He gave me grief because since Brian was gone, it was just him and Sofia. I told him I was sorry, but it wasn't like I had planned it that way. He said he understood and hoped that I felt better. Bastard.

Even though I still felt like shit, I went over to Elsa's. I figured she wasn't there, but it would be nice just to see her place. It seemed like it had been a while. When I got there, though, I saw something that I hadn't expected to see. The shades were drawn.

Chapter Twenty

It was the middle of the fucking afternoon! How could the shades be down?! She was supposed to be at work, it was Monday, Goddamn it! I stood against the building next to hers, right in front of the alley so I had a good view of her kitchen window and even that had the shades drawn! I tried to think that maybe there was a simple explanation. Maybe...she was sick and hadn't raised them or...maybe that guy was over and he was nailing her!

There wasn't anyone in the lobby of her building so I looked at the mailboxes and tried to find her bell. I wanted to ring it so I that I could interrupt whatever the hell may have been going on in the apartment. Just then, I heard this old lady walk out of an apartment. "Excuse me," she said and went to her mailbox. My bruises must have freaked her out a little because she was stole a few glances at me while she got her mail. Graham. Elsa Graham. It had to be there somewhere. Graham. E. Graham. "Can I help you?" the old lady croaked.

"Uh...no, thanks."

"Do you know somebody in this building?"

"Um…yeah. I mean…not…really."

"Then what are you doing here?"

"I…I've got a uh…a package. Outside. In my car. Van."

"Who's it for? I know everybody that lives here."

"You do?"

"Of course." She looked nervous which wasn't good. I tried to think of a name, any name but Elsa's. If I gave her Elsa's name, she'd probably tell me that she would sign for the package.

"Uh…Steve…Steve Giropolous?"

"Who?"

"Steve Giropolous?"

"There's nobody here by that name."

"Really?"

"What address are you looking for?"

"Nobody here by that name, huh? Okay. I guess I have the wrong address. Thanks for your help." I walked away and got to the door right as she started to say something.

There was nobody outside, so I ran down the alley to check her apartment from the back. The bedroom window was just like the kitchen, closed off. I didn't want to run the risk of being seen coming out of the alley, I went over the wall and slowly crawled down the other side and made my way to 24th Avenue.

Home was no good. I couldn't stand the thought of going back there. Instead, I walked all the way down to Astoria Park and sat on a bench near Hellgate Bridge. I don't remember how long I sat there, maybe an hour or two, but eventually I went to this Greek restaurant on the corner across the street and had one of those gyros. It didn't taste like anything. That wasn't a reflection on the chef, it was just that nothing would have had any taste to me at the time.

I hadn't smoked in years, but I went to the deli across from the restaurant and bought a pack of Marlboro's. The park was relatively empty, except for a few dog walkers and sun worshippers. Mr. Softee drove by and of course the truck played that stupid fucking ice-cream jingle and some kids ran toward him. Then out of nowhere, I saw her! She was walking a little blonde-haired boy up from the playground at the other end of the park toward Mr. Softee.

She wore jeans and a white tee shirt and of course, the sunglasses were a dead give away.

It was hard not to run up to her. Instead, I walked toward the ice-cream truck until I was almost right behind her. She was holding the little boy's hand and I heard him tell her three fucking times that he wanted a vanilla cone with sprinkles. There was a person who cut me off and stood right behind her, some fat woman who hadn't bothered to ask me if I was on line. She had this big purple dress on, kind of like a muumuu. A matching purple straw hat covered her head and she held a few dollars in her hand. I looked at her while her eyes ran over the menu posted on the window of the truck. For a second, I thought I saw her drool.

So I was behind this big fat bitch, trying to get a look at Elsa. There were a few kids in front of her and she bent down to say something to the kid. A breeze blew by just then and I couldn't help but close my eyes as I breathed in her perfume. As I did, I accidentally inched forward and bumped into the walking grape in front of me. She turned around and gave me a rude look, like I had interrupted her from the most important decision of her life. "You know, you could say excuse me," she said.

"What?" I asked her that because I couldn't believe that she had actually said what she had said.

"I said that you could have at least said excuse me for bumping into me."

"You've gotta be kiddin' lady."

"What?"

"You heard me tons of fun, you must be joking. Especially since you're the one who just wobbled on over here and planted your big fat ass in front of me and cut the line."

"How dare you talk to me like that?!"

"What like it's a fucking secret that you've got a big fat ass? That couldn't have been the first time you heard that. Lady, there are wrecking balls that don't weigh as much you do."

"You bastard!"

"Or cause as much damage when they move."

"Fuck you!" she screamed. At this point, everyone stopped what they were doing and looked at us. The guy in the Mr. Softee truck, the people on line, everyone.

"I wouldn't know where to begin to do that, ma'am. Or how to in your case. Jesus, I don't think Houdini could figure that one out. Not without a slide rule anyway." She hauled off to smack me, but I moved out of the way. "Oh I bet if I had been holding a fucking Twinkie you would've connected," I said. The kids laughed and the woman tried to swat me again, but I just moved. "You asshole!" she said.

I looked over at Elsa, and she held the kid closer. "Hey! What's going on there?" the guy in the truck said.

"This is your lucky day, man," I said, "you'll be out of ice cream by the time she's through with you. You'll be able to go home early. Of course, I feel sorry for the rest of the neighborhood kids who won't get any."

"Fucking asshole!" she was swinging wild now and had even dropped her money.

"Hey, I bet this is the best work out you've had in a while, huh?! What am I talking about?! I bet this is the only workout you've ever had!" The kids all "Oooed" at the same time. I just kept my distance from her. After one or two missed swings, she broke into tears and ran off. Well, trotted.

The kids looked at me and a few were still snickered. Elsa was standing there with her mouth open. When I got closer, she backed away a little with the kid and I noticed that she had a small scar on her upper lip. Not only that, but she had taken off her sunglasses.

Brown. Her eyes were brown. It wasn't even her.

Chapter Twenty-One

I walked back to the driveway and lifted myself up the wall to look at her windows. Shades were still down. My head started to hurt, so I lowered myself back down and wound up sitting in Hoyt Park again. A fat couple walked by and I thought about the lady I had insulted in Astoria Park. I had never done anything like that before. Truth be told, I didn't feel the least bit bad about it. It actually felt pretty good. The way I saw it, she had it coming. It was bad enough I had to put up with those assholes at work, I sure as hell wasn't going to do it on my own time. She cut me off and then had the balls to tell me how to respond after bumping into her?!

By 11 that night, I hadn't seen her and that's when I started to worry. For the past five hours I had alternated between the park and the back of her building via the driveway and there was no change in the place from what I could see. Well, from what I couldn't see, actually, since the shades hadn't moved from when I had seen them earlier that day. My headache had gotten worse and I tried to climb the fire escape, but I was still weak from the beating I took. Rather than risk falling off or getting caught, I just got down, sat by the trash for a while, and stared at her window.

A cat woke me at 2 in the morning. It meowed and looked at me with those green freaky eyes that cats have, almost like searchlights. The shades were still down and I was feeling sore from sleeping on the ground, so I walked out and got a cab on Astoria Boulevard.

I was too tired when I got home, so I waited until the next day to shower. When I got to work that morning, George threw a "good morning" out in the air when he passed by my cube on the way to his office. He had switched Sofia's schedule to compensate for Brian's absence until he found someone to replace Brian. His two week notice still hadn't been enough time for them to get someone else to take his place and the few people that had applied for the job weren't qualified, according to George. It wasn't surprising that people weren't lining up to get a position in Customer Service. I can't say I blamed them.

After talking to some guy in Maine who called to tell us that he felt Astor House was anti-Catholic because there weren't as many Catholic bibles on our shelves as there were others, it was time to go to lunch. At the pizzeria, Floyd had a million questions for me about why I looked all banged up and in no uncertain terms, I told him that it was really none of his business. He looked sheepishly at his slice and took a bite. I just kind of stared at mine. "Aren't you hungry?" he asked and I tried to ignore the glimpse of the chewed up piece in his mouth when he spoke.

"Not really."

"I cccan't believe I forgot my sandwich again. I feel ssso stupid."

"Really," I said.

"Aaand the train made me, uh, made me lllate this morning again so I...cccouldn't get breakfast."

"Yeah, that seems to happen a lot."

"You know, I –"

"Let me guess, you made your tuna fish sandwich this morning and then forgot it on the counter, right?"

"Um...yyyeah."

"It's nice to know that you can count on some things to be consistent, isn't it Fffloyd?" I got up and walked out of the pizzeria.

Back at my cube I took out a picture of her that I had printed out. There were several that I had printed and put up around my desk at home and a couple by my bed, but the one I carried with me was my favorite. It was the one I took of her sleeping. As I stared at her I kept thinking, *"What was she doing? What exactly was she doing?"* And more importantly, I wondered what exactly he was doing to her.

The phone rang and when I picked it up, some woman was asking where she could submit a request for a charitable donation. Without taking my eyes off the picture, I gave her the address. "Address it to Corporate Relations."

"Great, thanks. Anyone in particular?"

"No."

"Ok. Thanks ag-" I hung up before she finished, still looking at Elsa.

"Who's that?" George asked. I swiveled around in my chair and saw him standing over me, peering over my shoulder.

"A friend," I said and I put the picture in my shirt pocket.

"Hmm. Here, enter these letters in the database and give them back to me when you're done. By the way, I heard you on that last call. Let's try to pep it up." He tossed me a stack of miscellaneous letters from miscellaneous customers and tapped the blue index card with the company mission statement before he walked away. When he got back to his office, he shut the door. I stared at the door for a while and imagined myself kicking the damn thing open and the surprised look on his face as I threw the letters at him. Before he realized what happened, I pictured myself jumping on his desk and pissing on his computer. For good measure, I'd light the mission statement on fire like a draft card and let it drop on his floor.

That would have been sweet. *That* would have been pure.

I alternated that day between data entry and answering the phones. Sofia had her head in her hands most of the afternoon. One of the calls I got was from some guy out in Cleveland. The very first words out of his mouth were, "I'm going to sue you guys."

"Really?" I said, without really thinking.

"Yeah! Everybody's gonna hear about what happened to me today and by the time I'm done with you guys, you won't even have people going into your stores to ask for change."

"Sounds pretty serious, sir. Would you mind telling me what happened?"

"One of your managers, Kelly, told me to leave the store and also told me not to come back."

"She did? Which store was this?"

"Your store."

"Yes, I realize that you mean one of our stores, *sir*. But exactly which store of ours has a manager named Kelly in it who kicked you out and told you not to go back?"

"Are you being a wiseass with me? Are you? Because I'll take this all the way up to the president of the company if I have to, man. Don't mess with me!"

"No sir, I wasn't being a wiseass. I'm just trying to get all the facts."

"It was at your store on 92nd Street and 35th Avenue in Queens."

"I see, thanks. And uh, what happened?"

"I was in there browsing and this…bitch-"

"Sir, I'm going to have to ask you not to curse, please."

"Well, that's what she is."

"If you continue, I can't talk to you or help you."

"Fine, whatever. Anyway, Kelly comes up to me while I'm looking through the Poetry section and tells me that I have to leave."

"That's it?"

"Yup."

"So let me see if I understand this correctly. You were just browsing through our store, minding your own business when all of sudden, Kelly comes up to you and tells you to leave the store."

"That's right."

"Did she say why?

"No."

"Did you ask her?"

"No. She said that if I didn't leave right away, she'd call the police to escort me out."

"So she asked you to leave and not come back, seemingly for no reason, and you didn't ask why. She just picked you out of the blue."

"Yup."

"Interesting. Okay sir, let me look into this and we'll call you back."

After I got his information on where to call him back, I looked up the Region Manager for the area and called him on his cell phone. Before he even picked up, I already knew that the customer was full of shit and he was trying to make something out of a situation that he was embarrassed by. The Region Manager picked up the phone and I told him what happened. It turned out that he already knew about this. There were a few differences between the story he gave me and the store's version of events. First of all, the guy hadn't been in the Poetry section, he had been in the Sexuality section. The reason he was asked to leave was because he was opening some of the books with the illustrations in it and licking the pages. I guess Hilda been wrong after all.

After I gave the Region Manager the guy's contact information so he could follow up with the fucking pervert, I hung up and tried to concentrate on finishing the stack of letters. I took another look at Elsa's picture and remembered the last conversation we had. God, it was so great. I really thought that it would have brought us close and made us friends and…possibly more. It drove me nuts that I didn't know what she was doing. Even though I knew that she was probably with…that guy, I tried not to think about it. After all, he couldn't be that much different from the page-licking scumbag that had just called me. If he were, he wouldn't have manhandled her hard enough to have left a mark afterwards. Of course, he wouldn't care about something like that. That's the part that really pissed me off. He didn't care. None of them did. They just cared about themselves, about how they felt. They were all a bunch of egomaniacal, twisted fucking babies forever chasing after the nipple.

When five o'clock rolled around, I still hadn't finished with the letters. George must have noticed the time, because he came out of his office to ask me if I could stay until closing to help keep coverage. "You mean keep coverage until 6?"

"Yes. And that way, you can finish entering all the letters."

"Well sorry, George, but I can't do that."

"I see. Well, what about the rest of the week? Can you do that?"

"No, George, I can't. Especially not with this late notice. Maybe if you had talked to me about it sometime in the two weeks that Brian gave notice, something could have been arranged, but not like this. No."

"I'm asking this as a favor. It would help keep our team strong and our company represented professionally when they hear on our outgoing message that we are open Monday through Friday from 8 to 6."

"Oh, I understand, George," I said while I shut off my computer. "I understand completely. Believe me, I'm crystal clear on this. But it doesn't really change anything. See it's like I already said, I can't do it. Not with this late notice."

"I'm sorry to hear that, Everest."

"I'll bet you are," I snickered.

"Something on your mind, Everest? You have a problem you'd like to discuss?"

"Not especially, George."

"I ask because you just sound like you've got something on your mind and-"

"And we know that we can always come and talk to you about anything, right George?"

"Yes…that's right."

"I got the shit kicked out of me in an attempted mugging a few days ago, George. I had to call out yesterday to try and get some things in order. You took it as an annoyance. You didn't even ask me if I was okay this morning. Hell, it's the end of my shift today and you still haven't asked me how I'm feeling. So you'll forgive me if I'm not exactly up to the task of 'doing you a favor'."

On the train ride home, I thought about what I had said to George and that stupid look on his face as I had said it. I can't lie, it felt good! Hell, it felt fucking great! I had wanted to sound off on him for years except that I was always afraid of the ripple effects something like that would cause. For some reason though, that didn't bother me anymore. In fact, it was the last thing that I thought about. My first, second and third priority was finding out if Elsa was okay. Everything and everyone else could go fuck themselves as far as I was concerned.

She wasn't on the train ride home. I got off on Astoria Boulevard and when I got to the alley, I saw that her shades were up. When I got to her bedroom window, though, I found that she had locked it and I couldn't get in. As I peered into the room, everything looked the same as it had before. It didn't look like she was home, there weren't any lights on. After I took a couple of more pictures of her room with my phone, I climbed down and waited at Hoyt Park until I could see her. When midnight rolled around and she still hadn't shown up, I went home.

It was like that for the rest of the week. There was no sign of her on the train, no movement at her apartment. George barely spoke to me. He only addressed me when he had to and it was always very curt and direct. Floyd kept his distance from me as well. If he did forget his lunch that week, he certainly didn't eat at the pizzeria.

By the following Monday, I was a mess. I had pretty much spent the weekend between the park, the diner, and the trash behind her building. What's worse is that I probably not only looked like it, I probably smelled like it. To top it all off, I had been getting to work late. It was tough to drag myself out of bed. When I did, I would drink some orange juice while I stared at the Elsa wall I had made in my apartment. Since I couldn't find her, I had made copies of all the different pictures of her and put them up on the wall in my bedroom so she'd be the first thing I'd see in the morning and the last thing I'd see before going to bed at night. I'd get lost in all those shots, remembering each specific day that I took the pictures. Before I knew it, it was way past the time I needed to leave in order to get to work on time. That Monday was no different.

I bumped into Hilda on my out and she asked me how I was feeling. "I'm fine, Hilda, thanks. Late for work."

"I won't keep you then," she smiled, although it seemed like something was on her mind.

"What is it Hilda? Something I can do for you?"

"Well, I just wanted to ask you something."

"Yeah?" I said, irritated.

"The other night I was going to check in on you, but just before I knocked on your door I heard you talking. I thought maybe you had company so I didn't want to disturb you, but then I heard you cursing and getting a little loud. Then I heard what sounded like…well like maybe you were crying," she lowered her voice when she mentioned the crying.

Looking at her just then, I felt really bad. She was obviously concerned and wanted to make sure that I was okay, especially after what had happened when I got jumped. It seemed like a sweet, heartfelt sentiment and she was trying to be a good neighbor. "Well, Hilda, thanks. Thank you for your concern."

"Oh, you're welcome, I-"

"But in the future maybe you can just…focus on Cherry and MIND YOUR OWN DAMN BUSINESS!"

Immediately, she backed up and the look of shock on her face just made me angrier. At that moment, all I wanted was to test her resolve and throw her across the courtyard to see if she could still not be sour on people. There must've been something of that in my face because she quickly turned and hurried down the hall.

Chapter Twenty-Two

George wasn't in his office when I got to work. Sofia was already on the phone and waved at me when I passed by. After my computer came online and I settled in, I glanced over the phone messages that she and George had divided between us that day. There were eight of them that I would have to call back. The e-mails were a little heavy that morning. I was supposed to answer fifteen.

Joanne Edelsohn was in the break room when I walked in. "Oh, hi, Everest. How was your weekend?" she asked.

"Great, Joanne, just great."

"Good." She was preparing some coffee and I had to move around her to get a cup, a spoon and some sugar packets. God forbid she actually had to stop stirring and get out of the fucking way. I waved off the stench of her Chanel perfume and I think she saw me out of the corner of her eye. Smiling, I poured myself a cup. "So…how's Customer Service treating you?"

"How's it treating me? Oh just fine, thank you. You know we're just like the Maytag repair man. We sit around and haven't a thing to do all day because there's never anything that people find to complain about." She gave me a nervous laugh and told me to have

a good day.

"Oh, thank you. You be sure to have a good day too Joanne. Knock

'em dead out there!" She kind of looked at me funny before leaving.

When I got back to my desk, George still hadn't gotten back.

Sofia had just hung up and she asked me how I was doing. "Fine.

How have the phones been?"

"Not too bad, actually. One of the women who called over the

weekend left a really irate message on voicemail."

"Really? What else is new?"

"No, I mean, she was really pissed."

"What happened?"

"She didn't say. She was just talking really loudly and said that she

had just left one of the stores and was really disturbed by what she

found when she visited. She said that this bothered her so much that

she doesn't know if she'll ever go back and will start telling her

friends to do the same."

"I see. Oh, she'll be a real joy to talk to."

"You'll have to let me know."

"What do you mean? She's on my list?"

"First one. George asked me to give her to you."

"Oh he did, huh? Well, I guess our fearless leader must know what he's doing, right? I'll be sure to get right on it then."

I called the customer, she was out of Virginia, but there was no answer so I left a message on her answering machine. Sofia was on the phone when the other line rang so I picked it up. "Astor House Books, this is Everest."

"Who's this?"

"Everest! My name is Everest."

"Oh. Well my name is Judy Benson and I just wanted to call and let you know that I think you all need to go over your customer service at your store in Charlotte."

"What happened?"

"I was in there last night and I went up to the register and right there at eye level with a child was a *Maxim* magazine display with a naked woman on the cover."

"The woman was naked on the cover?"

"Yes."

"Well, ma'am, I've actually got a copy of the cover right here and I'm sorry to disagree with you but she's not naked."

"Oh well, she might as well be. She's topless!"

"Well…yes, but-"

"I mean granted, you can't see her breasts because her arms are covering it up and she's turned profile, but still. That is very inappropriate and I think you all should take that down."

"I understand how you feel, ma'am, and I'm sorry that you were upset by this."

"I don't want to hear that, I want to know if you're going to take this display down."

"Well, no."

"No?"

"The displays in the stores change and as I understand it, this one will be up until the end of next week."

"So, you don't care that you're exposing children to this smut?"

"No, that's not it at all, ma'am. We just-"

"I'm going to write a letter to the press, telling them how Astor House wants to pervert our children by putting up displays like this in their stores. I'm going to mount a campaign against your company and protest outside your stores until you stop exposing our children to this." She hung up before I had a chance to say anything.

I had been holding the picture of Elsa in my hands throughout the call, hoping that it would keep me calm. It wasn't working. Instead, I thought about that last time I saw her. She had a bruise on her leg. A *bruise*. He had soiled her already. He made her different from when I first saw her and that was really not sitting well with me. Maybe that's what was happening this whole week when I couldn't see her. Who knew what he had been doing to her? I wondered, *what if she needed help to get away from him? What if she was hurt and he wouldn't let her go and I couldn't help because I was answering calls from assholes like this lady all day long?* She had become the absolute best part of my day. Shit, she had become the best part of my fucking life! I began to think these horrible fucking thoughts. I kept picturing her cowering in a corner somewhere in her apartment with this guy sitting on her couch holding onto the neck of a bottle of beer while a cigarette dangled from his lips. God, I wanted to get my hands on him. The more I stared at her picture, the more it ate me up and the more I felt like I couldn't sit still. My mind went back to the night I got jumped and while I still harbored this immense anger at those idiots, I also felt this instant gratification when I remembered how I punched the bald guy in the balls. Was it wrong to also feel a slight thrill run down my spine when I thought about how Jimmy's bleeding head stained the sidewalk? At that moment, I would have given anything to have done the same to the guy who had bruised her.

My head was pounding and I felt this throbbing at my temples. The lady from Virginia called and Sofia picked it up. "Everest, it's that lady from this morning. She's on line one. Still sounds upset." My eyes got blurry for a second and I took a deep breath before answering the phone. I was sweating my ass off, but I took a sip of coffee anyway. "Hello, this is Everest."

"Are you the one who left a message on my answering machine? You're the one who called me back?"

"Yes, ma'am. I was returning your call."

"Yes, do you guys care at all about your customers?"

"Yes. Yes, we do."

"Well, I don't think so. I really don't think so. Not after the experience I just had over the weekend."

"I'm...sss...I'm sorry ma'am. Wh...what happened?"

"I'll tell you what happened. I spend a lot of money in your store and I went into your store here in Norfolk on Sunday and after standing in line at your café for five full minutes, I got to the front and your employee tells me that they can't make caramel frappucinos that day because they ran out of caramel. I actually had to go next door to The Java Bar and get it there. They had it and your store should have had it. It doesn't take a genius to see when you're running low on something, why didn't they order more? I always get my drink there on Sunday and this just ruined my whole day. Now what are you going to do about it to make me feel better about going back to your store because I don't know if I will."

It's kind of hard to describe what happened after that. All I know is that my hands were trembling and shaking Elsa's picture. There was this buzzing sound in my ears coming from somewhere and my head felt like it was going to explode. "Coffee?" I asked. "This...is...all about...coffee?"

I stood up and closed my eyes. Everything became very clear, suddenly. It was almost like a fog had lifted from my brain and after taking a really deep breath, I answered her. "I can't believe that this is what you're FUCKING CALLING ABOUT! This is what the urgency was about? You couldn't get you're precious fucking frappuccino yesterday from our store?! You got it from another store, so what's the fucking problem?! God, you're such a FUCKING BABY! That's what you are, ma'am. You're a whiny little bitch of a baby, ok? So you couldn't get a caramel frappu-fucking-ccino, BIG FUCKING DEAL! What are you, a child, you need everything you want at the moment you ask for it?! Do me and everyone else in your life a favor okay lady? SHUT THE FUCK UP! AND HERE, HERE'S YOUR FUCKING COFFEE!" I poured the rest of my cup over the phone and slammed down the receiver.

People were looking at me over the tops of their cubes. There was a weird kind of silence throughout the whole office. Fuck the proverbial pin, you could hear atoms splitting. I sat back down and put Elsa's picture in my shirt pocket. Sofia came over to me and ignored the calls that were coming in. "Uh, Everest?"

"Yeah?"

"Um…you okay?"

"Fine, thanks. Better than fine, in fact. I'm peachy keen, Sofia."

"I don't think so. Maybe you should, uh…not answer anymore calls today."

"You think?"

"It might be best, yeah."

"Okay, Sofia."

"Um, I'll be right back." I knew exactly where she was going. She was going to find George. In the meantime, I decided to answer some of the e-mails. The first one was from a customer who thought that we were selling too many books by Al Franken and not enough books from the Conservative party's point of view. Even the e-mail had that sarcastic tone that I could just imagine coming out of his mouth. *I can't believe that a company as big as Astor House would actually show itself to be partial to any political party. I am sure that this is just an oversight. Still, I wonder what the reason could be for this unbalanced display?*

Dear Sir,

You hit the nail right on the head! We <u>are</u> showing political partiality in our stores. It is our secret intent to bring down the conservative party in this country by stocking our stores only with left-wing titles. We figure that way, people won't have any other choice in the whole world but to buy them and then be converted to the Liberal party. But now you're on to us and you've blown our cover, so now we'll have to figure something else out. How clever of you! You should be commended sir, on your keen insight into the subversive tactics of the Leftist Party. We're a sneaky bunch, but I guess we just didn't get up early enough in the morning to fool you, now did we? Rats! Curses!

Thank you sir for writing us. Al Franken thanks you too. I guess we'll just have to fold up tents and move along. No hard feelings, though sir, really.

Oh and incidentally, get a fucking life you right wing prick!

Sincerely,

Customer Service

I don't think that I really meant to hit the "Send" button, I can't really be sure, but I had hit it anyway. It didn't really matter at that point. Honestly, it felt good. I mean it felt *really* good. It was like all of a sudden, a valve had been released and all this steam was set loose. Even my headache was getting better. I still had that buzzing in my ears, though.

I also realized that by answering the e-mails this way, I was getting them done a lot faster and therefore, I was increasing productivity. I knew George would like that. The next one was from a woman who wrote in that she couldn't believe that our stores let people sit in our cafes for hours just because they bought some coffee. *I went in there over the weekend and I couldn't get a seat because your policy doesn't let your employees ask people to move if they've been sitting there for hours without buying anything else except the coffee they purchased when they first got there. I had to*

leave after buying my latte! Now what are you prepared to do about
this?

This one was much easier. I didn't bother to try and spruce it up
at all or include a lot of bullshit.

Dear Valued Customer,

Go fuck yourself.

Love,

Customer Service

I liked that one so much that after I sent it, I copied it and used it
to answer all the other e-mails I had left. Fifteen e-mails answered
within five minutes. Sofia had pulled George out of whatever
meeting he was in and brought him over to my cube. Apparently,
she had told him what happened because his brow was already
wrinkled by the time he got there. "What's going on, Everest?" I
didn't answer him. Instead I just sat there and looked at him. "Um,
can I see you in my office?"

He closed the door and sat down at his desk. The image of me jumping up and pissing all over the place came back into my head and I let out a smirk. "You think this is funny? Sofia told me what you said in the last call. What was that all about?"

"I...I don't..."

"Talk to me, Everest. What the hell is going on with you lately?! You're coming in late, you're dressed like a slob and some people have even commented that there's a...an odor."

"What people?"

"Just...people. Let's leave it at that. Now what's going on? What's happening with you?"

"You know, George, I really don't...I...maybe, I think, I think I have to go."

"Everest, this is pretty serious. I mean, we're looking at possible termination here."

"Possible? I think it'll be pretty definite once you hear back from some of the other customers," I smiled.

"What? What does that mean?"

"Um...I finished all the e-mails you gave me."

Chapter Twenty-Three

Security escorted me out of the building. George told me to clear out my desk, but I didn't have any personal effects there, so I told him that that wouldn't be necessary. When they came, George and I were still sitting in his office, not saying anything. For the first time since I went to work for him, George was at a lack for words. He was responsible for what had happened, after all. That's the way that they higher ups would look at it. Customer Service was his department and everything we did was a reflection on him. I stood up and George told security that I was to be escorted out of the building and not permitted to return under any circumstances. I guess he thought I might come back with a shotgun or something. As entertaining as the thought was, I wouldn't even know where to get one.

I said goodbye to Sofia as we walked out. She was the one I actually felt bad for. Now, she would be the only one on the front lines. The bulk of the work in that department would fall on her shoulders. If she was skinny then, I guessed she was going to need an IV.

Instead of going home, I went to her office building in Midtown. I waited until lunch and then I watched carefully as the crowd came out. Every face was an irritation; everyone that passed by me was just some asshole who wasn't her. After a while, I kind of lost hope. I stayed there until well after five and didn't see her once. *"Where the fuck could she be?!"* I wondered.

I think I was talking out-loud because people kept looking at me and then edging away from me on the train. After Queensboro Plaza, Ben came on and made his usual request for money or a smile. When he came up to me, I showed him Elsa's picture. "Have you seen this lady recently?" He looked me up and down, trying to figure out if he should answer.

"No."

"But you've seen her before, right? I mean, you know who this is."

"I see a lot of people on the train, man."

"Yeah but not like this, not like her. Come on, she gave you a sandwich one day and I was standing next to her not too long ago when she gave you some money. Now, have you seen her?"

"It's like I said man, I see a lot of people on the train and lots of them give me money and food sometimes. Sorry I can't help you out." He started to walk away and I reached out and grabbed his arm.

"Listen to me! I know you know this woman. We both gave you money the last time I saw her and you even told us that you always get your best fucking smiles on this train. Remember?"
"Look man, get your hands off me. Now I said I don't know the lady so why don't you just back off." The other passengers were looking at us and I stepped a little closer to him. The smell that emanated from him could make anyone dizzy, but I didn't care. Grabbing him with both hands, I shoved him against the doors and looked right into his eyes. "If you don't tell me if you've seen her, I fucking swear to God that today will be the last time you'll ever see a 'beautiful smile' again," I said through gritted teeth. "Mister…please, I aint done nothin'. I aint seen nobody. Please mister, don't hurt me. I'm just trying to get by. Please mister, please." He started to cry. The train stopped and I let him go. He turned away and kept sobbing while everyone else just stared at me.

"WHAT ARE YOU LOOKING AT?!" I yelled, walking out of the car.

It was a long walk to her building, but since I had no cash on me and there wasn't an ATM around to save my life, I had to walk it. By the time I got to her building, it was already dark. Funny how fast time passes sometimes and you don't even realize it. I went over the wall and crouched by the garbage again. The shades were down again, so I got comfortable and waited. 7:05 PM. My life had undergone some pretty unexpected changes in those past few hours. I didn't know what I was going to do for work and chances were that I wouldn't get a favorable reference from Astor House. In a worse case scenario, I thought I would go back to being a waiter. None of that really mattered, though. Not at that moment. There was something not right happening and I wanted to help her.

The light came on suddenly. Well, not exactly suddenly, it was 8:30. I saw some shadows move slightly, but they were too far from the window make out. The blinds turned and someone other than Elsa was standing there. I crouched down lower and got closer to the trash to avoid being seen. The drawback was that I couldn't see him either, but for the moment, it would do. It was definitely a man, though. That much I was sure of.

Carefully, I took a peek and saw that he had turned the blinds back. He turned off the lights and a few minutes later, I saw the bathroom light go on. I figured that was my chance, so I quickly climbed up the fire escape, hoping that the other tenants wouldn't see or hear me, but not really caring if they did. It was hard to see inside, but not impossible. The jerk didn't turn the blinds back all the way and I was able to see through the slats.

The room was dark and the only light was coming from the bathroom inside. When I peered in, I saw her foot. It was…tied to the bedpost! So was the other one. She was naked and spread eagle on the bed. Naked. As I looked over her body, I saw that she was gagged and her hands were tied to the headboard. She was staring at the ceiling and moving her hands and feet. It looked like she was trying to break free!

Suddenly, she stopped moving. From inside the apartment, I heard him speak. While I wasn't able to make out what he was saying, I did hear a voice inside. Elsa moved a little more and saw me at the window when she turned her head. Her eyes went wide and she struggled even harder to get loose, but she couldn't break the binds. I heard the voice again and realized that I had better do something soon to get out of there so I sat down and smashed the window open by kicking it with both feet.

That's when all hell broke loose. As I climbed inside, the guy came rushing out of the bathroom while Elsa strained against the ropes and yelled through the gag tied around her mouth. It was Steve.

He stood there and stared at me in disbelief. Obviously, I must've had the same expression on my face. "Everest?" he asked. He was naked as well and had started to lose his erection. Steve. Steve had tied her up and had been using her the whole time! I felt like someone was taking a sledgehammer to my temples, but I managed to speak. "Steve. But...you...you're married. How...how did this...how do you even know her?"

"Everest, what the hell are you doing here?!" he asked, fumbling for his pants that were on the floor next to the bed.

"You're married!"

"What the fuck are you doing here?! What's going on?!"

"I don't under...what are you doing to her, Steve?"

"Everest, I'm going to ask you one more –"

"No! I asked you, Steve. What are you doing to her? YOU TELL ME WHAT'S GOING ON!"

"Goddamn it, Everest, I'm warning you. If you -"

"You met her on the train, didn't you? Just like I did," I looked at her, scared and worried on the bed. She looked too scared to move and I had guessed that it was because she didn't want him to hurt me like he had hurt her.

"You met her on the train," I said, looking back at him. "You followed her, found out where she lived, what time she leaves her apartment, what time she comes home and then you kidnapped her, didn't you?"

"What?" he looked over at Elsa.

"Don't look at her, you bastard! You don't get to look at her, you don't deserve to look at her!"

"Everest, you need to calm down."

"Goddamn it, Steve. I can't believe you. I can't believe this! You sick, twisted fuck! How could you do this to her? She's perfect, don't you understand, you dense motherfucker?! She's perfect and you're trying to break her! You've had her here this whole time, defiling her, haven't you? You've kept her tied up so she couldn't struggle against you, right?"

"Everest, what are you –"

"Well, I'm not going to let you do that. I WON'T!"

"I don't know what you're talking about," he said, calmly. I didn't understand how he could have acted so calmly when I had discovered what he was doing. When I looked at her again, she had tears running down her face and such a look of fear that it made me even angrier. He was standing in front of me half dressed, the one who had caused all her worst fears to come to life. I felt as if a damn had suddenly burst apart inside me and a rage was pouring through me that would only be satisfied by wrapping my hands around Steve's throat and squeezing the life out of him.

"I met her first, Steve! I met her first and you can't have her, understand?! YOU CAN'T HAVE HER!" I charged him and rammed him against the wall. In the background, I could hear Elsa screaming through the gag and shaking the headboard. We crashed against the dresser, then the nightstand, and fell to the floor. "You fuck! You sick motherfucker! How the fuck can you do this?! How the fuck can you do this to her?! I won't let you! YOU HEAR ME, YOU FUCK?!" We rolled around the ground and I had my hands around his neck, squeezing as hard as I could. He punched me in the face and broke my grip. As he got up to get away, I grabbed him by his ankle and pulled him toward me. He fell hard against the floor and I jumped on him from behind.

I can't remember anything else that I said or anything that he had said either. Somehow, he got me in a headlock on the ground at one point, but I punched him in the stomach and he let go. As soon as he did, I grabbed him in a half-nelson. He was really stronger than I thought, because after a few seconds he managed to stand up with me on his back. I held on tight, knowing that I couldn't afford to let him go. He kept trying to elbow me. While I kept my hold on to him, I ignored the pain in my body and squeezed even tighter, trying to get him back on the ground. Steve thrashed around until we slammed against the dresser one more time and then landed on the floor with me on top of him. When we landed, I felt something in his neck snap and he went limp.

I was panting and sweating and Elsa was still screaming. Steve had this empty look in his eyes and I could tell that he was dead. When I let him go, he lay against the ground and I checked for a pulse but couldn't find one. Elsa was still screaming.

I stared at him for a few seconds after I got up. The rage was gone and it felt good to see him dead, I have to admit. I know how that sounds, but it's true. It felt damn good. As I turned to her, she was still crying and struggling against the restraints. "Don't worry," I said and pointed at Steve. "He's dead. He can't hurt you anymore," I smiled. Taking one last look at Steve, I walked over and sat on the side of the bed, next to her. "Now…now we can be

together, finally. It's going to be great, Elsa. Just you…and me."
While I stroked her hair, I smiled and leaned over and looked at her
tear-stained face and glistening blue eyes. I kissed her forehead and
caressed her face, she didn't move. "Everything's going to be okay
now," I whispered. "You'll see. We're going to be so happy
together. I promise I'll spend the rest of my life making you happy."
I got up and watched her perfect naked body on the bed. As I undid
the binds at her feet, I felt so happy that I started to sing to her. I
sang Billy Joel's *She's Got a Way* and I felt myself get excited at the
thought that she would be soon be in my arms. The angst that I had
felt for so long would finally be over.

I had barely gotten her hands free when she pulled the gag from
her mouth and pushed past me, knocking me to the floor. "Get the
fuck off me you piece of shit! Steve! STEVE!" she screamed and
went over to him. Kneeling down beside him, she cradled his head
in her arms and cried. "Oh my God! Oh my God, I can't believe
this. Baby?!"

As I watched the scene play out in front of me, I stood up and slowly backed up to the broken window. My brain struggled to understand what was going on and I slumped against the wall almost as limply as Steve was on the floor. "Elsa?" I asked.

"Oh my God! What did you do? What the fuck did you do?!"

"He...he was hurting you. I...I wanted to...I wanted to save you."

"What the hell are you talking about, you sick fuck?!"

"Elsa, he's married. All he wanted was to...take you."

"I know he's married, you asshole, what fucking business is it of yours?!" I stared at her in disbelief. *She already knew?*

"No," I whispered as the tears formed in my eyes. Not her too. "Elsa." She...enjoyed the bruise and everything that had been involved with it? "But...but we were supposed to take care of each other," I said. "You're not like...them." But even as I said it, I knew that I was wrong. I had been wrong the whole time thinking that she was different. She was just like everyone else - false, dirty, disappointing. When this realization dawned on me, I remember feeling the rage build up again. All that time I had spent following her, seeking refuge in the very thought of her, worrying about her like an idiot! All that time, she was laughing and fucking Steve's brains out! She was no different than any of them, the people on the train, the ones that called, my own mother! It was too much for me to take in, I didn't want it to end that way!

I don't remember when, exactly, but I had gotten up and pulled her away from Steve. Throwing her to the floor, I held her wrists in my hands as she screamed. "Stop it!" I yelled. "STOP IT ELSA!" She struggled to get away, but I didn't want her to go. I thought that I could still save her and bring us together. "You can't be like him! You can't be like ANY of them! You're not, don't you get it?! You're better, you're sweeter, you're purer, Elsa. Don't let them take you," I begged.

"Get off me!" she shrieked.

"I won't let you! I won't let you be like them! We can be together, my love. The minute I saw you, I knew you were different. I fell for you the first time I saw you on the train. It was like Dante and Beatrice. Something…so real. It's beautiful, Elsa. Don't you see?"

"The only thing I see is that you're a pathetic, sick asshole! GET OFF ME!" she screamed, then kneed me in the balls and pushed me away.

When I fell on the floor next to her, she ran out of the room. I don't know if she remembered that she was naked, but she ran right to the door and out of the apartment. As I lay there and tried to catch my breath, it sounded like there was a lot of commotion out in the hallway. I guessed that the people in the building had heard the fight and had come out of their apartments. I was able to make out Elsa screaming and crying for someone to call the police and I heard someone shout that they were on their way.

A few minutes later, I managed to get on my hands and knees and crawl back toward the wall by the window. The rage had passed and my body had started to feel the aftermath of the night. As I closed my eyes, I let out a deep breath and I fought back the urge to cry. It had all been for nothing. All the pictures and the dreams were for nothing. I sat against the wall and looked at the picture she had on her desk of her and her family. I looked at her and thought about how beautiful she was. Maybe it was wrong of me to think that just then, I don't know.

It was 9:10 by my watch. Her broken clock read 8:54. Had I mention that already? Sixteen minutes. That's all it took. The whole thing was over in sixteen minutes. I looked over at the body, *his* body. There were cuts on the bottom of his feet. From the hallway, I could still hear Elsa crying. Although I tried to fight it, I was crying too. I heard her, but she was different that night. Not pure like before. Not *my* Elsa.

The sirens finally stopped outside the building. I didn't even try to get up, to get away. It would've been pointless. There was nothing waiting for me out there. I realized then there hadn't been anything out there for me in years. At least, not until I met *her* and that hadn't turned out well.

Elsa. Elsa Graham. The girl in the picture that I had in my shirt pocket when the cops got into the apartment. They took it away from me, of course. And I was told they took all the pictures I had of her at home, as well as my computer and cell phone. My lawyer had painted this picture of me as a broken man who never really had a chance after finding my mother dead. The psychiatrist that evaluated me agreed with him during his testimony. Maybe they were right, maybe my life would have been different if she hadn't killed herself. Honestly, I hadn't thought about it until it was brought up during the hearing.

I admit that the hardest part of those six months during the trial was when Elsa was called to testify. She broke down a few times during questioning and would never so much as glance in my direction. It turned out she had met Steve at a local bar a block from where she lived. Melissa sat there, barely able to keep her composure while Elsa testified. The last time I saw her was the day of the ruling. Among all the faces that filled the room and the people that took my picture for the news, Elsa's was the one that stood out to me the most, of course. As soon as they read the verdict, she wiped away a tear, put her sunglasses on and left the courtroom quickly before I was taken away.

When I got here they explained that the pictures had to be taken away and that it was for my own good and it would help me get better, but I didn't believe them; I still don't. Besides, what was the point in trying to get "better" when nothing out there is or has a hope

to be? George, Floyd, Hilda, all the customers, Ben...Elsa.

Everything that I left out there is still in the same shape as before

only they don't seem to know it. Maybe it's best to just stay in here.

At least here, most of us know we're sick.

I still ask every day, though. I ask about the pictures, about Elsa.

They never tell me anything.

64523543R00190

Made in the USA
Middletown, DE
14 February 2018

The Truth About Elves